FROM USA Today BESTSELLING AUTHOR

ERIN BEDFORD

IMPRISONED BY THE Vampires

HOUSE OF DURAND
BOOK NINE

Cover Design by TakeCover Designs

Editing by Makenzie Frazier

ALSO BY ERIN BEDFORD

The Underground
Chasing Rabbits
Chasing Cats
Chasing Princes
Chasing Shadows
Chasing Hearts

The Crimes of Alice
The Crimes of Alice
Hatter's Heart
Cheshire's Smile

The Mary Wiles Chronicles
Marked by Hell
Bound by Hell
Deceived by Hell
Tempted by Hell
Betrayed by Hell

Fairy Tale Bad Boys
Beauty and the Hunter
Wendy's Pirate
More Precious Than Gold

Starcrossed Dragons
Riding Lightning
Grinding Frost
Swallowing Fire
Pounding Earth

Curse of the Fairy Tales
Rapunzel Untamed
Rapunzel Unveiled
Rapunzel Unchained

The Beast of the Fae Court

Children of the Fallen
Death In Her Eyes
Fire In Her Blood

Her Angels
Heaven's Embrace
Heaven's A Beach
Heaven's Most Wanted

House of Durand
Indebted to the Vampires
Wanted by the Vampires
Protected by the Vampires
Embrace of the Vampires
Tempted by the Butler
Loved by the Vampires
Huntress of the Vampires
Judged by the Vampires
Imprisoned by the Vampires

Academy of Witches
Witching On A Star
As You Witch
Witch You Were Here
Just Witch It
Summer Witchin'

Wicked Crown
Little Morning Star
When Hell Freezes Over
To Hell With It

House of Van Helsing
Her Cross To Bear
Blood Betrayal

Granting Her Wish
Vampire CEO

ERIN BEDFORD

CHAPTER 1

Piper

OH GOD WHAT IS that smell? It's almost like a hot pile of garbage was rolled around in a roadkill carcass and topped with barbeque sauce.

I covered my nose and mouth at the smell, my eyes watering and my stomach rolling. Agnes came around the corner with a tray in her hands. The closer she came to me the more my stomach revolted until finally, I shoved myself up from my seat and found the nearby trash can.

Welp. There went my breakfast.

As I came back up, wiping my mouth with the washcloth I'd taken to keep with me, the tray clattered on the table a few feet away. I blinked up at the female vampire. Agnes was assigned to me the day I was brought into the council's 'safety.' They could call it whatever they wanted. I was a prisoner. They were using me to keep the Durands in line and it was working.

"Please," I croaked, waving my hand at the tray and turning my face away. "Take it away. I can't...I can't stand the smell."

Agnes huffed and grabbed the tray. "You didn't want the stew I brought you either. What do you want?" Agnes's patience with me was clearly wavering. Why they think a fifteenth century midwife was the way to go...

I contemplated what the baby wanted. It wanted to go home, that's what it wanted and I couldn't disagree. I was lucky that I was only three months along or I'd be in real trouble. I didn't know how the vampires thought I was going to give birth but I did not want it to be in this overly plush room. I needed a hospital with doctors and nurses and drugs! I didn't want to feel shit when I pushed this thing out of my vagina.

If only I could give birth like a giraffe. Silent, stoic, no pain evident as the gooey baby giraffe fell out of their vagina without any effort on the mom's part. Then she's all like, let's go time for tea or whatever giraffes did to socialize.

But that wasn't what Agnes meant.

Letting out a heavy sigh, I rolled my eyes up at the vampire. "How about something made this century?"

Agnes's nose curled up. "You mean something fried in grease?"

The very sound of the words made my stomach rumble in eagerness. "Yes," I pushed up straighter in my seat. "Preferably fries. Lots of fries. Maybe with some chili and cheese sauce?" My mouth watered at the very thought of it.

Agnes huffed and stalked out of the room. Whether or not she would actually bring me what I asked for is up to anyone's guess. I just hoped it wasn't anymore of her disgusting home remedies. I couldn't bear anymore of those tonics that tasted like whale's piss.

Leaning back in my chair, I tilted my head back on the head rest. What were the guys doing now? How much longer would I have to tolerate the 'safety' of the council?

Honestly, I was surprised the Hunter's Guild hadn't raised hell in all the time I've been gone. I knew Vincent was eager to get information from us about the council's whereabouts in exchange for mine and the Durands freedom from them. Unfortunately, I couldn't follow up on that promise just yet. The longer I was with the council the more I wanted to turn them all over to the hunters and let them all burn.

I pushed myself to my feet, my hand on my stomach. I walked through the lavish room the council had so graciously bestowed on me. It was garish and not to my taste. Though it seemed that the older the vampire, the more outrageous their tastes became. Every piece of furniture was carved out of red oak with depictions of snakes, birds, and other wild animals. The blankets were a brocade design of black, white and crimson. I could hardly stand to sleep in the bed with that much busyness happening on the top. Not to mention that I hadn't slept alone in quite a while. I missed the guys and I missed my home.

I wrapped my arms around myself and frowned. I needed to get out of here.

"Miss Durand," Tuma's smooth accented voice called my attention back to the open door of my room. The council member had a hand up to knock, a mocking attempt at giving me privacy.

They thought I didn't know they had cameras in the room and a guard at my door almost every moment of the day. The only times I don't are during the day when the halls are filled with the vampire council's minions. Stepping out that door on my own was like slitting my own throat and offering it up for any vampire to drink from.

"Tuma," I inclined my head at the dark-skinned vampire. "What do I owe the pleasure of your company today? Are you finally going to allow me to go home?"

Tuma tapped his cane on the marble floor and flashed a grin at me, his teeth so shockingly white that I wondered if they would glow in the dark. "Unfortunately, the threat of the Hunters Guild is far too high to allow you to return to your home. You must remain here with us for the time being."

I wrinkled my nose and tried not to speak what was on my mind. I'd had to learn the hard way that curbing my tongue would get me more with these creatures than my usual fiery passion that swayed the Durands. With careful consideration of my words I said, "I understand. I thank you for your protection and I know the others do as well. Have you heard from them?"

I'd been in the council's possession for over a month now and during that time I hadn't been allowed to see the others. I could talk to them on the phone — monitored by a council member of course or exchange letters, also read over by the council. No, there would be no sneaking around and making plans to escape without the council knowing, that was for sure.

Tuma nodded and withdrew his top hat from his head, holding it before him along with his cane. "Yes, your men have been busy keeping the Hunters Guild at bay. They try their best to keep them from finding out where we have hidden you. The gods know the hunters would love to get their hands on a baby born of two vampire servants. Could you imagine the kind of fighter they would create?"

I chewed on my lower lip and bobbed my head.

We had this discussion before. By being Antoine's human servants, Darren and I both had enhanced senses and speed. Individually we were almost as strong and fast as a vampire but combine us together? And you would have a vampire killing machine. Or at least that was the belief. No one seemed to know for sure what exactly would happen at our child's birth. For all we knew, it could come out being a regular old human. The longer I was in the council's hands, the more I wished it were so.

"Still…" I began trying to be polite with my words. Honey, Piper. You catch more flies with honey. "I would like to see them soon." I rubbed a hand over my stomach which had barely begun to extend. "I would hate for them to miss my pregnancy entirely. It's not every day that a vampire's servant has a child you know."

"And you will," Tuma stepped toward me, his hands open wide with a placating smile on his face. "We just have to be cautious right now. I assure you, when the time is right you will be reunited with your family. Please have patience for a little bit longer."

"Alright. If you say so," I took a deep breath and forced myself to say, "I trust your judgment."

Tuma grinned, his fangs gleaming in the light. "As you should. Now, I will let you rest. We don't want our mother to be getting too tired." He bowed at the waist before putting his top hat back on and pivoting on his heel.

Then I was alone.

I gave myself a moment, moving around the room as if nothing was wrong before casually walking over to the door and closing it firmly. Then I walked leisurely back toward my bed and laid down. Turning in the bed, I shoved my face into the pillow and screamed.

CHAPTER 2

Piper

I STOOD IN THE library, balancing precariously on the top of a ladder as I dusted the top shelf. I sang a random pop song under my breath not paying much mind to my surroundings.

I didn't know how long I'd been dusting but there was something soothing about it. Something simple. It was nice to have something so void of complexity and supernatural politics. Unlike the usual craziness of my life. Here, I could just be.

"You really shouldn't be up there in your condition."

I yipped and clutched the sides of the bookshelf, the ladder beneath me wobbling at my sudden movement. A hand settled on my lower back, steading me.

Once my heart stopped racing, I glared down at Antoine. "Did you really have to do that? There are better ways to announce your presence, you know."

Antoine hovered behind me as I cautiously made my way down the ladder.

Landing in front of him, I smacked a hand on the front of his grey three-piece suit. Which even in a dream was perfectly pristine and in place.

"Stop hovering. I'm not going to fall and break my neck in a dream."

Antoine inclined his head, his silvery white hair falling over his shoulder, his lips thinning. "Forgive me if my inability to protect you in real life has made me more than a little overprotective in our dream meetings."

I sighed and cupped the side of his pale face with my hand, peering into those pale blue eyes. "I know. I hate this too."

Antoine placed his hand over mine tugging me toward him. His other arm wrapped around my waist pressing me against the front of him. "You underestimate the reaction of the others. Hate is simply too weak of a word for how they are reacting. Marcus is practically biting at the bit, wanting to throw all caution to the wind and storm the castle doors so to speak." He narrowed his gaze on me. "And he is the least of my concerns."

I grimaced. Out of all seven of the Durand men, Marcus was the most stoic of them. For him to be pushing back at Antoine's orders, the others must really be losing their shit.

Fuck. Rayne.

The youngest and moodiest of the Durand with good reason, would be feeling not only his own distress about my captivity but everyone else's in the house. I hoped they were trying their best to keep their thoughts to themselves around him.

"Do not worry," Antoine murmured into my hair, holding me close to him. "You are far more precious to us than our own pride. The others will do their best to keep their own emotions in check."

I pursed my lips and rolled my eyes up to Antoine's face. "I'm not worried about you killing each other. I'm worried about you getting killed trying to get to me." I blew out a hard breath and pushed away from Antoine, wrapping my arms around my middle. "We don't know why exactly the council decided they were better at keeping me 'safe' than you guys would be. We don't even know what the end goal is. Not to forget that Vincent wants information from us about the council. Information I can't provide."

Antoine wrapped his fingers around my arm and led me out of the bookshelves and over to a couch that held more than one delicious memory. Instead of letting me sit on my own, Antoine pulled me into his lap so that his arms were on my thighs and his hand could rest on my swelling belly.

His fingers circled my navel as he spoke. "Vincent is aware of the situation."

I startled in his lap. "You told him I'm pregnant? You don't know what he will do with that information. We don't know what kind of abilities our child will have. You know that he will try to use it to turn it into one of his hunters. I can't believe you would tell him without consulting me first!" My voice went higher in pitch with each word.

Antoine stared at me without saying a word until I was done. Then gripped my chin between his thumb and forefinger. "Are you quite done?"

I scowled. "No. But go on."

"First of all, do not presume I have done anything that might put you, our child, or our family in danger. I am utterly disappointed you would even think of such a thing." He released my chin abruptly, his hand going to his tie, loosening it. "Secondly, Vincent does not know about your condition and will not learn about it from any of us. We will manage Vincent. You must handle the council and the precious cargo you are carrying. Give me your hands."

My hands automatically shot out before me of their own volition. Antoine wrapped the length of his tie around my hands pulling them tight enough that I couldn't escape but not so much that it bit into my hands.

"What do you think you are doing?" I stared down at my hands and then back up to Antoine, cocking a brow.

Antoine checked the knot before grabbing a hold of the loose ends and tugging me off of his lap and onto the couch. He spun me around so my back hit the couch cushions and I gasped. The skirt of my dress fell up my thighs, exposing a good portion of leg to him.

"You seem to have forgotten who the master is and who is the servant in this scenario." Antoine leaned over me, holding my hands above my head with one hand, his hair falling into a curtain around us.

I snorted. "When did you ever think I agreed to you being my master."

He rolled his hips against the junction between my thighs and a toe-curling friction found itself dancing across my moistened folds.

"I would imagine around the time you took the job." Antoine offered with another thrust of his hips.

I shook my head. "Nope. Not in the job description."

Antoine's mouth found the shell of my ear, his tongue sliding down the length of my neck. "Perhaps it was when I made you my human servant." His fangs teased the place where his mark would forever be embedded into my skin and my hips bucked against him.

"A technicality." I gasped, tugging at my bound hands. "I had to do it..."

"Had to?" Antoine purred against my neck before lowering down to the neckline of my dress. Riiiip. Antoine jerked the bodice in half baring my breasts to him.

"You could have imagined it away. You didn't have to rip it." I grumbled. I liked this dress. Even if it wasn't real.

Antoine peered up at me briefly to state, "Not nearly as satisfying," before he struck. His fangs sliced into the flesh of my breast and though it was a dream I felt every second of it as if he were in the bedroom with me on the other side of town where the vampire council were holding me captive.

His mouth sucked on my breast while his hand snuck between us. Jerking at the skirt of my dress, he pushed it up my waist. Those long fingers found their way between my thighs and though he had preferred to rip the dress, my panties disappeared.

Moaning and bucking against his hand, I tugged with more earnestness at my hands, wanting to touch him more than anything.

"Please..." I cried out.

Antoine flicked my clit and lifted his head from my breast, licking my blood from his lips. "Yes?" His fingers pumped into me over and over so that I couldn't get a word out. "Tell me, Piper. What is it you want?"

"P...please," I tried again, whimpering. "Let me go."

Antoine stopped. His hand was gone.

I cried out and thrashed at the sudden loss of his hand. I'd been so close. So close to release. I needed it. I needed him. All of them. Like I needed to breathe. I was suffocating here. Moments away from slashing my way through the vampires until I reached freedom and sweet, sweet release.

My body flipped and my knees were shoved up and apart. Antoine growled into my ear, "I will never let you go," then thrust inside of me.

With one hand on my hip and the other holding my hands tightly above me, Antoine shoved his way inside, hitting me exactly where I needed it most.

My cheek pressed into the side of the couch, the material biting into my skin. Every shift of Antoine's hips brought me higher and higher. My legs shook with effort and my clit ached for release.

I could only imagine what I looked like laying in my bed alone while being fucked within an inch of my life inside my mind. Was I moaning like a bitch in heat? Could they smell the scent of my arousal beneath the sheets? Would I scream out when I finally reached orgasm?

"Stop thinking," Antoine ordered with an extra hard thrust of his hips. "Be here with me."

I swallowed down my scream and tried to do as he wanted. The vampire council had taken so much from me I wouldn't let them have this too. Except that was easier said than done. Once I had thought about how I looked from the outside I found myself curbing my moans. Biting my lips to hold back my screams. Trying to hold myself still so as to not give away what was happening.

Antoine was having none of that.

We shifted again this time my hands, still bound, were thrown over his neck as he guided me up and down on his lap. The rest of my dress disappeared and Antoine positioned us in just the right way that my swollen center rubbed against his lower abdomen as he thrust back inside of me.

My eyes closed tightly, my head falling back.

"No."

My eyes snapped open.

"Look at me." Antoine's command swept through my body and it was hard not to obey. I still didn't understand how his powers still worked in the dream world. Was it because of our bond or his abilities were just that strong?

The intensity of his gaze on mine made everything heightened and everything tightened.

"Tell me what I want to hear and I'll let you come." Antoine murmured against my lips.

"In your dreams," I panted and jerked him closer by my bound hands until our lips met.

I could taste the tang of my blood on his tongue and it only served to spur me on. Then it was me who was lifting myself by my arms and slamming myself back down on him. To my delight, Antoine groaned into my mouth.

"Piper," Antoine said into my mouth. "You have undone me." His hands tightened on my hips and seconds before he grunted one last command slipped out of me. "Now."

The tight ball that had been growing with every touch, every kiss, suddenly exploded. A screamed ripped through my throat and I did not care who the fuck heard it.

When I reluctantly came down, I leaned my forehead against Antoine's, our breath mingling together. "Aren't the guys jealous that you are able to see me like this and they can't?"

Antoine shrugged a shoulder nonchalantly. "They wish for you to be well taken care of and since we are unable to be there in person, we do what we can."

I grinned and rolled my eyes. "How convenient for you."

"It is a burden I must bear." Antoine answered with all seriousness.

I snorted and pushed to get off of him. Antoine grabbed me by the waist and held me there.

I held my hands up. "I'm free now. See?" His tie was gone from my wrists and back around his prim and proper neck.

"Are you though?" His lips curved up in a knowing smile.

I leaned in to kiss him. "Never."

Before I could land my lips on his, Antoine stiffened and his face turned as if to talk to someone and then I was falling through the air and woke up in the middle of my bed, the clear evidence of my release soaking my thighs and panties.

I stared down at my lonely bed for a moment, my heart catching in my throat before forcing myself to swallow it down. I got out of the bed and marched to the bathroom to clean up.

CHAPTER 3

Rayne

THE CONSISTENT TAPPING OF feet on the floor combined with the sighs and grunts coming from the other vampires in the room were just shy of driving me insane. Not to forget the roar of thoughts pushing at my brain.

What is going on in there?

Is Piper okay? Are they feeding her?

I'm going to march down there and break down the door. They can't stop all of us, if only we...

"Shut up already!" I snarled at the room, unable to take it any longer.

"I am sorry, *mon beau*. We are having quite a time controlling our thoughts." Wynn dragged a hand through his dark curls and sank further into his chair. The others nodded their heads in consensus around the sitting room.

I leaned my head against the fireplace mantel, closing my eyes against the words pouring in. "I don't think I can do this anymore."

"Don't say that, Rayne." Drake leaned forward on the couch, his hands clasped in front of him. His large bulging muscles making him look ridiculous all curled over himself. "We're all struggling here. And can you say that Piper isn't worth it?"

"And what about the baby?" Allister, Drake's twin, jumped in, usually the less vocal of the two. "Can you really give up Piper because of this?"

I dropped my hand and stared at him. "I don't mean leaving Piper. I mean, you assholes. I can't stand to be in the same room with you for two more seconds or my brain is going to explode. I am having a hard enough time dealing with this on my own, let alone listening to you worrying and whining like a bunch of babies." I jerked my arm toward them, pacing back and forth before the fireplace. "I just...I need a break." Shaking my head, I stalked toward the door.

Marcus stepped out of my way, him being the only one who wasn't driving me nuts with his constant thoughts though they were still there. Even he was worried for our girl.

Before I could make my exit Antoine appeared in the doorway, stopping me in my tracks.

Everyone crowded in behind me, their thoughts whirling so hard that I stumbled in place. Glaring at them, I focused on Antoine and tried to push the voices out. "What happened? Is Piper okay?"

Antoine ushered us back. Reluctantly the others filed back into the room, anxiously taking their seats once more. I couldn't sit. I needed to know what was going on. Then I had to get the hell out of there. I needed space. Or I didn't know what I was going to do.

"Don't leave us in suspense," Drake growled, his knee shaking relentlessly. "How is she?"

Antoine took his place in the tallest chair in the room. He took his time sitting down and crossing one leg over the other. He adjusted his tie and cleared his throat.

"Come the fuck on already!" Allister jumped to his feet.

Everyone's head jerked toward the vampire before Wynn threw his hand toward Allister. "What he said!"

Antoine waited patiently for everyone to calm down or at least as calm as they could be in this situation. I tried to peek into his head but the bastard was closed tighter than Drake's ass.

"Piper," Antoine began lacing his fingers over his knee. "Misses you all. She is distraught as we knew she would be, but otherwise she is doing well."

"And did you find this out before or after you fucked the living daylights out of her?" I scowled, crossing my arms over my chest and glowering at him.

The others looked from me to Antione and waited.

Antoine, never one to be frazzled, leveled his gaze on me. "Before, if you must know."

Drake groaned and threw himself back on the couch. "It's bad enough that you get to see her in your dreams, now you get to be inside her too? Fuck, I knew I should have been the one to claim her."

"Woah, woah now," I stepped up to the couch. "If anyone was going to claim her it was going to be me."

"And why would you think that, *mon ami?*" Wynn stroked his jaw with his finger and thumb, an intense look in his eyes. "I hope you do not think because you were the first one to experience her sweet folds that means you hold claim to her. I do not think Piper would like such a reasoning, do you?"

"I for one do not care for it," Darren said from the hall door. Darren adjusted his gloves and folded his hands before him, his suit even more pristine than usual. "I'm sure that Piper would love to know that you are all so concerned about who is seeing to her needs in the bedroom over her physical condition."

Drake snorted. "Oh, fuck off."

Allister rolled his eyes at his brother and patted him on the back. "Come on, Drake. Let's go take a walk. Let the grownups discuss things."

Drake shot a patronizing look at his brother. Then got up with him and left.

Wynn sighed and shifted out of his seat. "I should probably check in with Vincent. He has done nothing but pester us since Piper went underground."

I scoffed and threw myself down on the couch, my arms going behind my head. "That's a nice way to say it. Went underground. Not imprisoned by the vampire council. Not forced to stay away from her family because it's for the safety of her and the baby. Oh, yea. She went underground."

Marcus sniffed audibly, earning a look from Antoine.

"I am just as concerned as any of you," Antoine began, tapping his face with his fingertips. "Unfortunately, this is not something we can rush into. We have pressure coming from all sides and all of them have to do with Piper. We have to be careful how we handle this."

"Why don't we just get Vincent to help us?" I pointed out, able to finally relax and hear my own thoughts after half the room left.

"What do you mean?" Darren stepped further into the room, stopping just behind Antoine's chair. "Why would we tell Vincent?"

"If we tell Vincent where the council is then they will take them out and we can get Piper back," I explained feeling a bit proud of myself.

Marcus shook his head. "That will not work."

I dropped my arms to the couch and asked, "Why not? Vincent wants the council dead, we want the council dead, it's a win-win."

"Not for Piper it isn't." Darren explained. "Or for us."

My eyebrows scrunched together. "Why do you say that? It's not like they know about Piper's pregnancy. And when we deliver them to the council, they will let Piper out of her deal and we are home free."

"Pretty to think so," Antoine mused. "You are assuming that Vincent is a man of his word. What makes you think he would give up his best hunter when he could keep her and then what will happen when Piper begins to show? I think he will notice a bulging belly."

I shrugged. "We kill him too then."

"That's all good and well but the problem is that we are missing the how," Antoine pointed out with a stiff lip.

He had me there.

I couldn't think of a way that got us all what we wanted without getting any of us killed or Piper even further enslaved to the Guild.

Maybe there was something we were missing? Something that would make all of this better with a snap of my fingers. I just wish I knew what the hell it was!

"Anyway," I sighed and pushed up out of my seat to stand. "I need to get out of this house. If I have to listen to the thoughts of you all for one more moment, I'm either going to stake you all or myself."

"Actually," Antoine stopped me with the word. "Piper did express concern about you in particular."

I arched my brow. "She did? Why so?"

"Because of this very reason. Your gift may be causing you undue grief from the amount of stress we are all under. Perhaps you should take some time alone to sort out your thoughts? It may be prudent for you to keep your head during this strenuous time."

I shook my head, the auburn lengths of my bangs falling into my face. I really needed to get a haircut soon. "I can't just leave you all. I can handle it. I just need to practice blocking more."

Antoine inclined his head. "If you need anything, do not hesitate to ask. We do not have enough room to worry about you as well as Piper."

"Yeah, I think I just need a stiff drink," I stepped between the couch and his chair. "And maybe a sharp piece of wood."

CHAPTER 4

Darren

MARCUS LEFT SHORTLY AFTER Rayne, leaving me alone with Antoine.

Placing my hands on Antoine's stiff shoulders, I worked my fingers into the muscles beneath his suit jacket. Rayne and the others had many good points and I couldn't argue with any of them. I myself wanted nothing more than to steal Piper away and hide out on some faraway land so no one could find us. Except they would. The council and the hunters all had their ways.

We'd never be safe for long and then we would have to run again. And I didn't want that for Piper or my child.

My child. Wow. That has a strange ring to it.

While the likelihood of Piper being pregnant by anyone else but me was almost nonexistent, in fact it had never been heard of before, it was hard to believe that I had created a life. I never in my wildest dreams, even before Antoine made me his human servant, thought I would be a father. It would be mind-blowing had we not had bigger issues to deal with.

Antoine picked up my hand, stopping it from rubbing his shoulder. I paused the other one. "I have not seen you wear your gloves in quite a while." He traced his fingers along the line of my white gloves.

I held my hand still while he inspected them. "I suppose they comfort me."

Antoine hummed, still staring at my gloved hand. Then he pinched the tip of the material of my middle finger and pulled the glove down my hand. Tucking the glove into the front pocket of his suit jacket, he drew my hand against the curve of his cheek and then pressed his lips to the flesh of my palm.

I stood still unsure of what he was doing. It was unlike Antoine to be so affectionate.

Especially in a public part of the house. I didn't know if I wanted it to end or for him to continue.

Antoine's mouth found the pulse of my wrist, his tongue flicking out to lick it. I sucked in a hard breath, a jolt of pleasure going straight to my cock.

"What are you doing, master?" There was a quaver in my voice I had not heard in a long time.

Without looking up from what he was doing, Antoine answered, "I am distracting you from your worries."

Antoine tugged on my hand urging me around the chair. I knelt before him and peered up at him confused. "Isn't that my job, master?"

Leaning closer, Antoine's long fingers slid into the lengths of my slicked back hair gripping the black locks in his grasp.

"Do you think to tell me what I can and cannot do?" He snarled, bending my head back enough that it twinged slightly.

"Of course not, master." I gasped and forced myself to hold still. The sharp tug on my hair making me even harder.

A small smile played on Antoine's lips and he released me. "If only our Piper conceded so easily as you did. Why do you think she loathes to call me master? Is it such a hardship?"

I swallowed thickly and breathed out, "She is her own being. If she was anything other than a proud and stubborn little thing, I do not think the rest of us would have fallen so easily for her."

Antoine arched a pale brow. "You think so?"

I tried to find my words. "If she had been like all the other maids we have employed. Wynn and perhaps a few others would have fucked her and then you would have fired her."

"And why do you think our lovely Piper has lasted this long? We have all had her." He stroked his fingers along the side of my face.

I shivered.

"And yet..." Antoine continued, "here she is, pregnant with your child and bound to me forever. Curious how things work out."

"Yes," I panted, his fingers finding their way to my lower lip. He stroked his thumb across it and my mouth fell open for him. The urge to lick my lips was savage pounding against my head. I knew I couldn't though. Not without Antoine's permission. If I wanted this to lead to where I wanted it to, then I had to play the game.

"How does that make you feel?" Antoine inquired, those icy blue-eyed locking onto mine.

I started to answer and then stopped. I wasn't sure what I was answering.

How *did* I feel right now? Like I was going to come in my pants like a thirteen-year-old boy seeing his first pair of breasts.

Or was Antoine asking how I felt about Piper having my baby? Which was something I hadn't let myself think much about yet. Everything I loved in my life had been taken from me. It was only a matter of time before Antoine and Piper would be next. And with our track record that could be any day now. I couldn't let myself feel anything for the unborn child yet. Not when our future was so uncertain.

Instead of answering him, I reached for his belt.

"What do you think you are doing?" Antoine mused not stopping me but the bite in his voice told me he wasn't happy.

"My job," I retorted, purposely leaving off the master part.

Antoine grabbed my hands in his, holding them tight enough to pinch. "I don't remember giving you permission to touch me."

For the first time in the long years, I had served Antoine, I jerked away from him. His startled expression almost stopped me from what I had to say next but I did it anyway.

"So, Piper can touch you whenever she wants but I have to have permission?" I snarled while shoving to my feet. "I have been nothing but loyal and faithful to you from the moment you marked me and I am not worthy enough to touch you when I want? How is that fair?"

Antoine stared up at me, his mouth agape. I think I have made him speechless for the first time in his life. I'd have patted myself on the back for the very achievement had all my worries not crawled up my throat, bearing down on me like an executioner with an ax.

"Where is this coming from, Darren?" Antoine did not stand up from his seat, his hands falling to the arms of the chair. "I thought you were happy with our arrangement."

"Well, maybe I'm not." I snatched my glove from his coat pocket and shoved my fingers back inside, missing it the first two times before getting it right the last time. "Maybe I don't want to be treated like a pet you have to keep happy so you can fuck it whenever you want."

Antoine's brows furrowed and I knew I had pushed it too far. He stood abruptly from the chair.

I backed away from him slowly, my hands up between us.

"If I have made you unhappy then I would be more than happy to hear your grievances. However…" Antoine stalked toward me until my back touched the door leading to the dining room. "Seeing as we are bound together and I can feel everything you are feeling. I suggest you cut the shit as Piper would say and tell me what's really the matter."

Forcing myself from cowering, I stared Antoine straight in the face. "I'll tell you when you get Piper back."

Antoine stopped in place for a moment and then shook his head with a laugh of disbelief. "You have become far too bold since Piper has come to be with us."

"I would not say that is a bad thing." I retorted with a frown. I would not be laughed at!

Antoine shook his head again slightly and stepped toward me. I froze in place as he took my face between his hands and kissed me firmly on the lips. After a moment, I allowed myself to kiss him back. This is what I needed. This is what I wanted. No thinking. No questions. Just this.

To my dismay, Antoine wasn't having it. He withdrew from the kiss and smiled. It was a forlorn type of smile that made my heart clench in my chest.

"There are many things we both want. Unfortunately, at this time neither of us can have it. I am sorry my friend if I have caused you any distress. I will do my best to atone in the future. But I cannot do it as of now." Antoine stepped away from me and walked out of the room without another word.

Dumbfounded, I stayed in place for a long moment. It wasn't until Wynn appeared in the doorway of the living area that I snapped back into myself.

"Well, it sounds like you had about as much fun as I did talking to Vincent," Wynn commented as he strolled into the room. His shoulders were more droopy than usual. The feline grace in his step a bit more stiff.

"I take it the talk did not go well?"

Wynn scoffed and threw himself down on the couch, his legs sprawling out across the length of it. "If you think getting a threatening message from his second in command is going well, then yes it went splendidly." He paused for a moment, his eyes staring off at nothing. "I think we are being watched."

I finally moved away from the doorway. "You do?"

Wynn turned his gaze toward me. "They've noticed Piper isn't around. Or not showing herself outside of the house or in the windows. They're suspicious enough as it is. I do not know how we are going to keep her absence a secret much longer."

I frowned hard stroking my jaw as I tried to think. We needed more time. We needed a way to keep the hunters off our back until we could get Piper away from the council. How though?

Then I had it.

"What?" Wynn shot up from his lounging position. "What's that look about?"

"I think I may know a way to get the hunters off our backs. At least for a little bit," I explained to him while I started to take note of what I needed to do to make my plan work. "Let me make a few calls and I'll fill everyone in at once."

Wynn laid back on the couch and tossed an arm over his eyes. "You better make it fast. We only have a few days before Vincent himself comes to check on her. And if we don't have Piper back in our custody then or even a plan, then we're going to be in deep shit."

I let out a hard laugh. "How could we sink any deeper than we already are?"

CHAPTER 5

Piper

BORING. PAGE FLIP. BORING. Page flip. Borrrring.

I snapped the book shut and tossed it across the room. The book hit the wall with a thump. I usually wouldn't be so violent with a book but I was going crazy. I could not stand one more minute in this room. If I didn't get out of here soon then I was going to do something even more violent.

To my vicious delight, Agnes appeared at the door with a bored expression on her face. I could relate.

"Are you alright? We heard a loud thump." Her gaze circled the room before zeroing in on me.

I jumped out of my chair and stalked across the room. "No, I'm not okay. I'm bored. I'm tired of just staring at these four walls."

"Master Tuma insists that it is for your own safety —"

"Fuck that!" I growled, getting into Agnes's face. "I'm not a vampire. I'm human. I need sunlight. I need fresh air. I can't just sit in this room for the next seven months or I will go insane!" Seeing I wasn't getting through to her, my eyes skittered around the room and found the *What to Expect When You're Expecting* book. "And...and see," I grabbed the book and shoved it at her. "All the books say that for me to have a healthy pregnancy I need exercise and fresh air. If you keep me in here the baby won't develop right."

Agnes stared at me with uncertainty. "I will discuss it with Master Tuma. Until then," she gave me a pointed look. "No more throwing things."

I grinned at her innocently. "Of course not."

When Agnes left, I turned about the room and clasped my hands together with glee. With any luck, Agnes will listen and I will get to go outside! Which in itself was a win in my book but it would also be a great opportunity to find a way out of here.

I didn't get to see a lot of the house they were keeping me in. In fact, I didn't even think the guys knew exactly where I was. Supposedly, it was for my protection. Though, I'm not sure how they got that by the guys. Especially not Antoine.

There weren't any windows in my room and as far as I knew, I could be in the basement or the attic. The one time I'd tried to leave the room they had put me in, there had been Caleb with his creepy ass bored expression. The next day the door was locked and it had been from then on.

I didn't know how I let myself get talked into this. I scrubbed a hand over my face and stretched my back. The political mess we were in was stressing me out. No way that was good for the baby.

Sighing, I threw myself down on the couch and cupped my swelling stomach. It wasn't very big yet. Barely there at all really but I swear I'd felt it move already.

Could I call the baby an it?

I didn't know its gender yet so I suppose it didn't matter. I was more worried about what kind of abilities the baby would have than what gender it was. Was it bad that I hoped the baby was nothing more than an ordinary child?

Blowing out a breath between my lips, I stared up at the ceiling. God, didn't I wish I had my cell phone. There were so many things I wanted to look up. Someone out there had to have gotten knocked up by a human servant. I couldn't be the first one in all of time.

My brows furrowed.

Maybe there was one and they hid from the others because of this very reason. They didn't want the council to imprison them even if it was for their own good.

I wondered if I could get the guys to look into it. Next time I have a dream visit from Antoine, I'd tell him to —

The bedroom door opened once more. Agnes appeared in the doorway, her face pinched and a wry press of her lips. "Master Tuma has agreed to allow you to walk about the courtyard."

I hopped off the couch and threw my arms up in the air with a yippee.

"But!" Agnes cut my cheering off with a stern look. "You may only go outside with someone else. During the night," she seemed reluctant to finish the sentence. "I will escort you around the courtyard. A human servant or guard will escort you during the day."

Bobbing my head, I skipped toward her with a grin so big it hurt my cheeks. "Of course, of course. I get it. For my safety and all. Can we go now?"

"However," Agnes held up a finger with a sharp glare. "If you try to escape or cause any kind of disturbance in any way, your outside privileges will be taken away and you will have to suffice with what this room provides you." She said the last part with a smug grin as if she knew that I would fuck it up.

I did plan to fuck it up. I just didn't plan to get caught.

Of course, I didn't say this to Agnes, I put on a contrite look and crossed my heart with my fingers. "Cross my heart and hope to die."

Agnes snorted and turned her back on me, leaving the door open wide as she muttered, "You may by the end of it all."

Ignoring her thinly veiled threat, I happily followed after her.

We walked down a hallway that was about as dimly lit as a tomb. Vampires didn't need much light so I supposed it was normal for them. I didn't envy their human servants though. Just squinting in this myself was making my eyes ache.

An idea came to mind. An awful idea.

Maybe they didn't keep it this dim on purpose. Maybe this was all for my benefit. Or rather disadvantage. They were trying to make it so that I couldn't figure out where I was going on my own by making it so that I couldn't see more than three feet in front of me.

Well, if that was the plan, they were doing a good fucking job of it.

Still, I tried my best to keep track of where we were going. Down the hall, to the right, down a flight of stairs, another right, then a left and then we were outside.

I stopped right outside the door and just breathed in the fresh air. Each lungful of air was like a little burst of happiness in each and every cell in my body.

Agnes turned to me with an impatient scowl. "Are you coming? Or did you change your mind and we should go back?" She cocked a brow with a smirk.

I hurried across the courtyard with a panicked frown. "No, no. I'm coming. Just enjoying the air."

Agnes wrinkled her nose and stared up at nothing. "Breathing. Not something I miss."

I frowned. "But vampires breathe."

Turning her back to me, Agnes scanned the courtyard. No doubt checking for any ways for me to escape. "Not because we have to. Very few things can kill us." She gave me a knowing look at that. "You should know. Weren't you a hunter?"

I shrugged my shoulders. "One does what one has to to survive."

Agnes stared at me curiously with a murmur, "Yes, one does."

I walked along a stone path, trailing my hands along the bushes and plants, hoping that I looked like I was just enjoying the freedom. My eyes however were searching every part of the courtyard, looking for possible exits, weak points that could be exploited. Anything that I could use to my advantage.

Soon I found out that while I had gotten out of the room, I hadn't left my cage. The courtyard had only one door, the one we entered. The area, while large and full of plants and in any other circumstances a gorgeous fountain, was not what I needed. At that moment though, I would give it all up for a boring old wall I could climb. This was one of those stupid kinds of courtyards that were smack dab in the middle of the house.

Useful to those who had pets but about as useful to me as sunblock to a vampire.

"Not what you were expecting?" Agnes asked beside me with a smugness in her voice.

I spun around and faced her, a radiant smile plastered on my face. "No, it's great! Wonderful even." I turned around in place, staring with my mouth agape at the high walls of the building. No way I could climb those and not plummet to my death. "So, I get to come out here every day? Whenever I want?"

Agnes eyeballed me carefully. "Yes, as long as someone is available to escort you." When she didn't find what she was looking for she harrumphed and bobbed her head, lacing her fingers before her. "We can't have you wandering into the wrong part of the house and getting hurt now, can we?"

I nodded absently, still scanning the area for any way that I could use this to my advantage.

Agnes was quiet for a moment and then asked with a bit of uncertainty. "Is there anything else about human births that I should know about?"

"Huh?" I glanced away from the trees I was debating on climbing and back to my jailer. "About human births?"

"Yes," Agnes tucked her hands into the pockets of her apron and frowned. "I can agree that many things have changed since I was a midwife and if I am to make sure you are well taken care of and there are no complications then I need to be more up to date on the latest studies."

"Oh," I arched my brow and peered at her for a moment. Then a thought came to me. "You know…" I saddled up next to her with a sly smile. "There are all kinds of videos and such I could show you, lots of information about delivering babies in this day in age. If only I had my phone…" I tried not to be too eager as I casually laid out the bait.

Agnes was full on thinking about what she could do with that information no doubt. She probably hadn't even thought to get more up to date with her skills until now. I mean, why would she need to? If she suspected I wanted my phone for anything other than to help her and my child out she didn't mention it and I tried to be on my best behavior the rest of the time I was in the courtyard. Perhaps she'd be too curious herself to think straight about it and get me my phone. One could only hope.

CHAPTER 6

Wynn

WE WERE ALL GATHERED in the dining room where Darren was about to tell us his plan to keep Vincent off our backs. When I had messaged everyone about Darren's plan, they were all eager to get back to the house as quickly as possible.

Even Antoine had taken a break from his constant paperwork to sit and hear what his servant had to say. There was an odd tension between the two of them when he came into the room, but I only had enough energy to deal with one thing right now and that was focusing on getting Piper back.

Darren stood before the group with his hands clasped behind his back and waited patiently for us all to get settled.

"What's this all about a plan?" Drake threw himself down on the couch, throwing his legs up on the coffee table. Darren gave the vampire a scowl which prompted Drake to drop his feet.

"If you would be patient Master Drake then I will tell you all in a moment. We are just waiting for..." the back doorbell rang "...that. Excuse me." Darren marched across the room and out the door toward the kitchen.

"Do you know what all this is about?" Drake turned to Antoine, his knee bouncing in place.

Antoine did not turn his gaze to our brother, his gaze focused where his servant had left seconds ago. "No, I am not privy to every thought Darren has."

"Ooooo," Drake chuckled. "Someone get into a fight with their boyfriend?" Drake bumped his shoulder against his brother who shook his head at him in disappointment.

Seeing the expression on Antoine's face made me finally speak up. "I would advise you to keep your comments to yourself." Shifting in my seat, I sighed and stared off at the far corner where I'd first met Piper. It seemed like it was only yesterday she was breaking things and causing a panic in our quiet home. Strangely, not much has changed. "We are all on edge right now and we don't need to be fighting amongst ourselves."

Drake snorted and threw his feet back up on the coffee table. "Whatever. I'm just trying to lighten the mood. It's not every day that Darren has Antoine's panties in a twist. It's usually Piper."

Everyone was quiet for a moment at the mention of our noticeably absent lover.

"Yeah," Rayne breathed out, leaning forward with his elbows on his knees. "I'd give anything to fight with her again."

A rude sound came from Marcus and everyone turned his way.

"Do you have something to add, my stoic friend?" I gestured at him with a tight frown. "By all means, please share."

Marcus pushed off the wall by the mantle and glowered at the group. "You are acting as if she has died. When we are just one fight away from getting her back. If we would gather ourselves, we could breach the —"

"Marcus." Antoine's voice rang out throughout the room, causing all of us to still. "We have discussed this before. We will not go charging into an unknown place and put Piper's life in danger. Knowing the council, they may very well decide she and the baby are better off dead than in the hands of the hunter's guild." He leveled a look at all of us, the pulsating push of his power demanding we do his will pinched at my mind. "We must all have patience."

Just then Darren walked in with...Piper? I sniffed the air and narrowed my eyes. Wait...no that's not Piper.

"What the hell is this about?" Rayne growled, pushing up from his seat to stalk toward the blonde imposter. "You think you can just replace Piper like that with this...this..." he gestured at the woman who gave Rayne a flat look. "Phony?"

"Quite eloquently put Rayne," Antoine stated with a dry air, his own eyes looking over this new addition. "Darren," he addressed the butler who turned his gaze toward his master though there was a bit of a sting in that look that usually wasn't there. "Please explain this young lady's part in all this." He gestured to the woman and then around the room.

"Yes," I interjected. "Please tell us. Who is this woman and why does she look like Piper?"

Darren placed a hand on the fake Piper's shoulder. "This is Angelica. She's a shape shifting witch."

Angelica grinned and wiggled her fingers at us. "Hey ya'll," A strange southern accent came out of Piper's mouth.

"I hired Angelica to pose as Piper until we can find a solution for the Vampire Guild's constant inquiries."

Drake snorted. "Anyone with a nose will know that's not Piper."

"We don't need them to get close enough to smell her," Darren pointed out. "Just so that the guild believes she's alive and well."

Curiosity getting the best of me, I shoved off of my seat and approached the woman. Confidence poured from her until I was inches away and then there it was. That hint of fear and uncertainty flashed across her eyes.

"Are you afraid of us, Angelica?" I purred, picking up a piece of her blonde hair, the ends of it curled the way Piper usually would style.

Angelica licked her lips, her eyes dilating as she breathed out, "N...no."

"How do you expect to be able to play the part if you cannot stand for us to be this close to you?" I continued, wrapping my arm around her waist and pulling her against my front.

Rayne grunted in protest but I ignored him.

"You will have to play the part of our beau and that will require you to be quite close with us." I dipped my face down to her neck, teasing but not taking a taste. I would never do that to Piper.

"I...I...I don't know." Angelica stuttered out.

"Enough, Wynn," Antoine commanded, his powers pushing on me slightly.

I dropped my arms and stepped back from her.

Angelica blinked rapidly letting out a shaky breath.

Turning to Darren, I inclined my head. "She will be adequate but if anyone gets too close too long, they will know that this is not Piper. She isn't comfortable enough with vampires to pull off Piper's relationship with us."

"Correct you are," Antoine turned his gaze onto the fake Piper making her flinch back. "However..." he gazed around the room, touching each of my brothers in turn. "I believe we may be able to pull this off." He paused for a moment and then his gaze became laser sharp. "No, we will pull this off. For Piper's sake." Antoine brushed his thumb across his lower lip and then uncrossed his legs and stood from his chair. "Darren."

The butler snapped to attention. "Yes, master."

Antoine gestured toward Angelica. "You will take Piper — everyone should refer to her as such now — and show her around the house. Tell her what you can about the situation and what Piper would normally be doing."

Darren nodded and took Angelica — I mean, Piper — by the elbow and led her out of the room.

Allister spoke from his seat on the couch, his hands clasped before him. "And what should we do?"

"What would you normally do," Antoine answered, his eyes trailing after Darren's back.

Drake chuckled. "Well, I would normally be trying to distract Piper by shoving her up against the wall and ramming her —"

"Then find something else to do." Antoine shot a glare at Drake. "Rayne."

The redhead eyed Antoine with a scowl. His arms crossed over his chest as he propped himself up on the arm of the couch. "Yeah."

I wondered if Antoine would call Rayne out on his tone of voice like he usually would. Antoine was too distracted by other things it seemed to care.

"I need you to use your computer skills to figure out where Tuma is holding Piper. He couldn't have gone too far. He would want to keep an eye on us as well."

Rayne arched a brow and then nodded. "Sure. I can do that."

Antione didn't say anything for a moment and started toward the door Darren left through before pausing. "We don't want to put undue worry on Piper's shoulders. She has come through for us many times, now it is our turn to save her...and our child."

"What about Vincent?" I reminded Antoine, leaning an arm on the fireplace. "He will want to speak to Piper eventually. Do you think this..." I languidly rotated my wrist in the direction of the door. "...will be able to fool him? She couldn't even fool us."

"Vincent does not have as close of a relationship with Piper as we have." Antoine pursed his lips together, tucking his hands into his pocket. "We should facilitate a meeting with Vincent sooner rather than later. He has already no doubt begun to suspect something is amiss. I will leave that task to you."

Grimacing, I nodded. "Very well. However, I would also like to try something else that will give us all an opportunity to speak with Piper. We cannot let her think you are the only one distraught by her imprisonment."

Antoine flicked his hair over his shoulder and bobbed his head. "Do as you wish."

I frowned.

It was unlike Antoine to simply accept my plan without asking for more details. Still, I would not look a gift horse in the mouth.

CHAPTER 7

Piper

I WOKE THE NEXT morning from a loud knock on my door. The door burst open before I could even sit up in bed.

Two men came in — human from the smell of them — carrying a large flat screen TV. Agnes strode in after them, her brows furrowed and her mouth pinched together tightly.

Throwing my legs over the bed, I scrambled out of it and toward where the men were setting the television up. "What's all this?" Thankfully, I had chosen to wear a full set of pajamas to bed this time. It would have been funny — not for me — if I'd only worn a tank top and panties to bed like usual. Though, the way the men were keeping their gazes firmly away from me made me think I could have been prancing around naked and they wouldn't have looked.

Agnes looked from the men to me. "Unfortunately, I could not get your phone for you but when I asked Master Tuma about learning more about the modern human birthing experience, he agreed to give us this monstrosity."

Trying to repress my emotions regarding my phone, I snorted and laughed. "For someone who has lived for centuries you are quite behind on the times. What have you been doing all this time?"

Agnes grimaced. "I've been busy."

I crossed my arms under my chest, which was getting bigger than I liked. "So, what exactly am I supposed to do with this?" I flopped down on the couch and propped my feet up, watching the men attach the wires and program the controller.

"You wanted to teach me about human pregnancy." Agnes reminded me and gestured toward the television. "This is the best I could do."

I wrinkled my nose at the T.V. "Well, I guess we could watch some documentaries or something. Do you have any streaming services?"

"Streaming services?" Agnes frowned.

One of the men answered without turning to me. "We have all the services. If you need anything else just ask." He sat the controller down on the coffee table and he and his friend stalked out the door.

"Well..." I picked up the remote, surveying the buttons available, "they were friendly."

"Peons," Agnes provided and stepped closer to the television. "Humans who serve the vampires."

I cocked my head to the side. "They aren't human servants?"

Agnes shook her head, her graying hair bouncing with the movement. "No. We have many humans that serve us without being blood bound."

"Why?" I asked before being able to stop myself.

"Why what?"

I put my legs down and sat up straighter. "Why would they help you? Aren't they scared of you?"

"Are you scared of the Durands?" she shot back, moving over to the couch and taking a seat on the edge of the cushion next to me.

Agnes never sat down around me. It was almost as if she didn't trust me. Now she sat next to me as if she hadn't been tiptoeing around me since the day, she was assigned to watch me.

I shifted in my seat, pulling my legs up on the couch to face her. "Maybe at first." I thought back to when I first found out the Durands were vampires and laughed, a short sound almost a scoff. "Definitely at first. But it was more of what they were than who they were. I didn't understand..." I trailed off, staring at the wall behind Agnes.

I might not have understood what the Durands were at the time. It didn't take me long to figure it out. They weren't like the others. They didn't thrive on the pain of others. The need to feed was a necessity not something they languish in like their maker, Boris, and that asshole Valentine had.

Flinching at the memory of Valentine, I shook my head and gave Agnes a wry smile. "But obviously, I'm good with it now." I stroked a hand over my stomach and sank back against the couch arm.

Inclining her head, Agnes gestured toward the television. "Well, what should we start with? I will leave it to you. You're the expert it seems."

Ignoring the sarcasm in her voice, I flicked on the television.

Let's get this over with.

***

After hours of blood and guts and screaming — and that was just the birthing we watched — I needed a break. It was getting close to dawn now so Agnes excused herself for the day leaving me with some rando human servant to walk me around the courtyard.

The escort they gave me was kind of a meathead. Over muscled and silent even when he moved. He almost reminded me of Marcus. A pang of misery hit me in the heart.

Clearing my throat, I shot a look over at my escort. "So, are you going to say anything?"

The guy made a humming sound but didn't answer.

Annoyed, I walked around the fountain in the middle of the courtyard and glowered. "That's not really an answer. Are you just going to trail after me like a little dog because your master said so? Don't you have your own thoughts? Your own voice?"

"Don't bother with him."

I jerked around to a nearby window. The only window open inside the courtyard. I knew all of them only opened into more of the mansion and I shouldn't get my hopes up but a part of me saw an open window and thought, freedom.

Odette sat on the edge of the window, her flouncy skirt filling up most of the space. She held a doll in her hands, combing its hair absently while staring down at me.

Stepping toward the window, I squinted up at her. "Why not?"

"None of the human servants will help you. They're all bound to Tuma or Caleb. They won't talk unless allowed and they are under strict orders not to interact with you."

"None of them are bound to you?" I didn't know why I asked but it just came out of me. I should have turned on my heels and walked out of the courtyard the moment Odette appeared. Out of all the council members Odette was the creepiest. I didn't know if it was the way she talked or if it was the fact that she was a few hundred-year-old vampire stuck in a child's body that freaked me out the most.

Odette sighed longingly. "No. They won't let me turn anyone anymore."

"Why not?"

She held her doll up and held it over the edge of the windowsill. With a bored look she dropped the doll to the ground, the sound of it shattering echoed through the courtyard. Without a thought she flipped her legs over the side of the window and dropped out, her little Mary Jane's crushing the glass beneath her feet.

"Oh, I see." I didn't really but also didn't want to have this conversation anymore. In fact, I had the sudden urge to be anywhere but near here. I pivoted on my heel ready to make for the door but she was quicker than me. Odette's little hand slid into mine, squeezing it tight.

"Don't go." Odette commanded in that little sing-song voice of hers. "Stay and talk to me."

I licked my lips and swallowed hard. "What do you want to talk about?"

She giggled and bounced around to the front of me, before throwing her arms around my waist. I tried not to stiffen as she hugged me. Pushing against my need to rip the girl's head off, I patted her head awkwardly.

Leaning back from me, Odette stared down at my stomach. "I can hear its heartbeat."

"You can?" I arched my brow. "I'm not surprised your hearing is much better than mine."

When she released me, I pushed back the urge to sigh. I didn't want this kid anywhere near my baby.

"How does it feel?"

I placed my hand on my stomach and stepped back, feigning like I needed a moment to think about it. "Hmmm. I don't know. It's different. But a good different."

"My mommy was pregnant," Odette spouted out, suddenly her fangs flashing in a grin. "Before I ate her."

I gulped and forced a smile. "Oh yeah? Did you have any siblings?"

Odette shrugged. "Not after that. I was an only child and wanted to stay that way. Mommy didn't listen." She said it in such a matter-of-fact way that it made me nauseous.

This fucking kid. If I had a stake, I'd kill her on the spot.

I bobbed my head and blinked. "I get it. I hated my siblings too. I wish I'd been an only child."

"I could be your child." Odette beamed up at me, rocking on her heels.

Taken aback, I threw my head back and laughed. "I think that would be a bit hard."

"Why not?" She pouted, pushing her lip out and batting her lashes at me. "I like you. Don't you like me?"

"Of course, I do." I pushed my smile hard until it hurt. "For starters, you're way older than me and isn't a mom supposed to be the older one?"

Odette frowned, her little brow furrowing in thought. "Oh, yeah." Then giggled. "Then I can be your mommy."

I opened my mouth to find a reason why she shouldn't be.

"Odette. That's enough."

Saved by the vampire.

Now wasn't that getting old.

Caleb stepped into the courtyard. "It's time for bed."

The sun was beginning to rise. The light touched the top of the building on the west side. I hadn't realized it was getting so late. Or rather early.

"But Caleb, I want to play some more." Odette stomped her foot on the ground, her tiny fingers curled into fists.

Caleb's expression didn't change at all as he calmly stood by the doorway. "Odette, you know it's past your bedtime. Aren't you tired?"

Odette paused and then spun around and jumped back into the window. "Good night, Piper!"

I stiffened and then called back, "Night."

My gaze shifted back to where Caleb stood. He gave me a once over and then nodded before turning on his heels and leaving.

"Maybe I should have just stayed in my room." I said out loud.

"Ain't that the fucking truth."

I snorted and smirked at the human servant. "Oh, that makes you finally speak up?" I shook my head and started for the door. "Come on, chatterbox. Let's get out of here."

CHAPTER 8

Rayne

HUNCHED OVER MY COMPUTER, I typed so hard that the keys threatened to break beneath my fingertips. I'd been searching for Piper's location for weeks now and I haven't come across anything I could use to find her.

The door slammed open, smacking the wall behind it. Plaster fell on the floor with a crackle.

Drake stalked into my room with the energy of a freight train. "Please tell me you found her."

I scowled and gestured at my computer. "Do you think I would be sitting here in bed when I could be downstairs sleeping if I had found anything?"

His boots stomped across the room until he threw himself down on the end of my bed. I grabbed my computer and yelled, "Hey, watch it. Do you know how much this thing costs?"

Drake rolled his eyes and put his arms behind his head. "Not like you couldn't buy another one. Don't be such a baby."

I kicked my foot out at him, knocking his shoulder. "I'm not the baby. You are. I'm not the one who came barging into your room demanding answers."

Closing his eyes, Drake didn't even retaliate for me hitting him. "Right."

Pursing my lips, I stared down at him. Something wasn't right here.

Opening my mind, I zeroed in on Drake's thoughts. Before I could hear anything, Drake said, "Don't go poking around in my head. If you want to know something, ask."

I grunted and clipped my computer closed. "What do you want?"

"I told you, where's Piper?"

Shaking my head, I dragged my hand through the long pieces of red noting that I needed a haircut soon. "If that's all you wanted you would have just waited for our next meeting tonight. So…" I urged and then nudged him with my foot again to get his attention. "What's up?"

"Allister is being annoying. I needed to get away from him." Drake muttered, turning on his side so that his back was to me.

"Then why don't you go to your room?" I sat my computer to the side and watched the muscles flex in his back. The urge to read his mind was hard to resist.

"Because that stupid witch is in there." Drake snorted and air quoted. "Cleaning." He sat up and turned to me. "That woman wouldn't know how to clean if her life depended on it. You know I saw her using the toilet cleaner on the hallway floor?"

My nose wrinkled. "Ew."

"Yeah. And she ruined my favorite shirt by putting it in the wash." Drake's fingers curled into fists and pounded against his knees. "I'm half tempted just to snap her neck and be done with it. Deliver her body to the vampire guild so they'll get off our case."

I huffed. "Like that would work. That would just make them try to break the deal they had with Piper to leave us alone."

Drake blew out a hard breath. "Yeah, we're stuck between a rock and a hard place and there's no one we can kill to fix it."

I pursed my lips. "Maybe that's the problem. Everyone is so focused on killing each other that now the only way that we are going to get out of this situation is if they all just drop dead on their own."

"I wish. We'd need a miracle for that to happen." Drake shoved himself up and off the bed and twisted from one side to the other grunting as he stretched. "Well, I guess I'll go see if I can stomach Allister's whining."

"Good luck." I told him, picking my computer back up.

Drake snorted. "If he mysteriously ends up with a stake through his heart, you'll know who did it."

I chuckled as the door shut.

Everyone was on edge but it said something when the twins were driving each other nuts. I hoped that we could all stand it a little bit longer.

Leaning back against the headboard of my bed, I closed my eyes for a moment, reaching my powers out. I'd tried every day several times a day since Piper was taken, searching for Piper's brain signature. I stretched it until my head hurt and it snapped back like a rubber band.

Fuck. Piper, where are you?

I opened my eyes and lifted the top of my computer up. Well, back to the grindstone.

I'd find out where they were keeping her if it was the last thing I did.

The door to my bedroom opened again and I shifted in the bed. My eyes fluttered slightly at the noise. A familiar scent filled my nose. Through groggy eyes I saw Piper's silhouette.

"Hey baby, I missed you." I held my arms out to her from the bed. A moment later Piper's soft form pressed against me, settling into my embrace. I sighed and snuggled against her, burying my face in her hair.

Piper pressed her body close to mine, throwing one leg over my hip and another between mine. My lips twitched at the movement. Someone was feeling frisky.

Sliding my hand down her back, I cupped her ass in my hands and ground her hard against my growing erection. Piper moaned and arched into me. "That's it. You feel so good in my arms. I can't wait to get a taste of you again. I've missed you so much."

Piper's mouth slid over my jawline and then up my chin pulling my mouth to hers in a savage kiss. Wanting to savor every bit of her, I grasped the back of her head and angled her mouth, shoving my tongue between her lips to taste every inch of her, searching for the sweet taste of Piper.

My brows furrowed.

Cinnamon and…ash?

That couldn't be right.

Reaching my thoughts out, I touched Piper's mind.

Oh my god, I'm kissing a vampire. An honest to God vampire. Wait until the girls back at the coven hear about this.

Wait…is it fucked up to bang someone while glamoured as someone else?

Oh! Who the fuck cares. He's so fucking hot. I can feel his huge cock against me. This will be totally worth it!

It all came back to me then. I was searching for Piper on the computer. I must have fallen asleep. When Angelina came in I must have mistaken her for Piper because of my half-asleep state.

That didn't explain why Angelina came to me when she did.

I shoved her off of me and on to the floor with a snarl, flashing my fangs at her. "What the fuck are you doing in here Angelina?"

Angelina's eyes on Piper's face widened, startled and then suddenly struck with fear. She scrambled up off the floor, her hands before her as she backed away.

"Hey now, wait. You're the one who asked me to come to you. I never asked for you to start getting up all on me now." Angelina argued back with her southern accent coming out instead of the Piper voice she'd been using.

"Yes, that was my mistake." I climbed off the bed and stalked after her, pointing a finger at her. "But you went along with it. And yes, it is fucked up to try to screw someone while pretending to be their girlfriend."

"I'm so sorry." Angelica's eyes watered, her hands clasped in front of her. "I didn't mean anything by it. I just wanted to know what it was like for her. You know, I'm pretending to be her. This beautiful woman who somehow got all of you amazing men to fall in love with her. I mean, what is so special about her? Is her vagina magic or something?" The growl I let out made her stumble into a nearby chair. "I get it. I get it. I'm sorry it won't happen again. I promise."

"You're damn right it won't happen again," my voice rose with every word. "Because you'll be lucky to leave this house alive let alone keep this job."

Angelica let out a little squeal of terror and scurried to the door. "Get away from me. I'll turn you into…into a frog!"

I strode out of the room after her shouting, "Not if I eat you first!"

"What is the meaning of this?" Antoine's voice snapped my attention away from the sniveling witch. "Rayne. You cannot eat the help. We've been over this. And you," he asked Angelica with more of a calm manner than I felt. "What did you do?"

"I'll tell you what she did," I crossed my arms over my chest, my skin crawling from the very act of touching her. I couldn't stand to think what would have happened if we had gone any further. I wanted to scrub myself clean until my skin bled.

"Rayne."

My eyes stayed on the witch, the animalistic urge to rip her throat out almost too much for me to bear.

"Rayne," Antoine tried again, this time using his powers to command me. "Look at me, Rayne."

I tried to fight it but, in the end, I looked away from Angelica to Antoine. "What? She violated me. Tried to take advantage of me by using her glamour as Piper. She needs to go."

Antoine stared at me for a moment and then to Angelica. "Is this true? Did you do what Rayne has accused you of?"

Angelica licked her lips, her chin trembling as her eyes darted from me to Antoine and back. "I...I...it's not untrue. But it was just a misunderstanding." Angelica knelt on her knees toward Antoine. "He invited me into his bed. I thought he knew that it was me. That he just missed Piper enough to want something like her even if it wasn't really her."

I scoffed. "Like I am that pathetic."

"More men than you know are exactly that." Angelica shot back. "Where do you think I work for a living?" She sniffed, lifting her nose up in the air. "The club I work at caters to those types of men. The very ones who want to pretend. Either they've lost someone or they want someone they can't have. I give it to them."

I gaped at her. "Are you saying you're a prostitute?" I blinked at her and then over to Antoine. "Darren brought us a prostitute."

Silent for a moment, Antoine tucked his hands into his pockets and sighed. "Well, this is certainly an unexpected situation." His phone buzzed in his pocket. Antoine ignored it. "Angelica, what you did was completely disrespectful and your profession aside, something I will be discussing with my servant extensively, however...this isn't something we can just ignore. We cannot have an instance like this happening again."

"It won't." Angelica shook her head vehemently. "I promise. I'll stay away. I won't touch any of you."

"Very good. We —" Antoine's phone buzzed again. This time he pulled the phone out and glanced down at the screen. His face tightened. "— actually, scratch that. We may need you to touch us very intimately."

"What?" I stepped toward him. "Antoine what the fuck? I don't want this woman anywhere near me."

Antoine leveled me with a look. "Vincent is on his way."

CHAPTER 9

Antoine

THE DOORBELL RANG THROUGHOUT the house, making me tense.

This was it. We would find out if Angelica's glamour worked or not in the next few minutes.

"I thought you were taking care of Vincent," I addressed Wynn with an impatient scowl. "Having him come here to see Piper is not what I would call taking care of it."

Wynn lounged on the couch with one arm thrown over the shoulder and the other over the back. "I am doing as you asked, *mon ami.* I told him that Piper was indisposed but he could only take so much distraction. We cannot very well keep Piper sick forever. They know she is your servant. The fact that they believed me about her sickness is a miracle in itself."

"Why is he coming here now then?" Rayne growled, his arms over his chest. Every few moments he would glare at Angelica, making the witch shift uncomfortably.

"Rayne," I blinked at him, not bothering to push my power at him. "Stop making Piper uncomfortable."

Rayne's lip curled up and his nostrils flared. "Then maybe *Piper* should keep her hands to herself. Maybe *Piper* should do her job and not make other people uncomfortable."

Wynn brows rose. "Is there something I missed?"

"There is no time to discuss it right now." I waved him off, crossing my leg over the other while shifting toward Rayne. "I understand your feelings but you must think about Piper, the real Piper," I cut him off before he could make a snarky remark. "We

83

need this to work or we risk putting all of us in danger. Do you want that?"

Rayne's face tightened until it resembled an old potato and then he blew out a long breath and sank down into his chair. "Fine. I will put the incident behind me...for now." He gave Angelica a pointed look and then nodded at me. "For Piper's sake."

"Good." Lifting a hand up, I gestured toward Darren, who stood waiting in a corner of the room. "You may answer the door now."

Thankfully, only Wynn and Rayne would be available for this meeting.

The twins were downstairs sleeping. The twins were fighting and exhausted themselves to the point that they were in a coma-like state until dark. I would be concerned for them except in this case it was to a benefit for us. I didn't need to worry about them trying to tear each other's heads off when we should be focusing on keeping Piper safe.

Marcus had been up the last few days, doing what he did best. Finding information. While Rayne searched for Piper through the internet, Marcus was hunting down any possible leads to the council's whereabouts through their flunkies. There had to be someone out there that would know where the council was dwelling with Piper. They couldn't have just disappeared.

"What are we going to tell him?" Rayne murmured low enough that I could hear him but not the hunter's guild president coming our way.

"Do not worry. We are prepared for this." I stood from my chair and greeted Vincent with open arms and a twitch of my lips. "Welcome to our home. We weren't expecting to see you so soon, Vincent."

"Well, you know me. I'm a busy man. I have to check in on my investments." Vincent didn't try to shake my hand, his hands firmly tucked into his pockets. He grinned widely, not a care in the world making him worry about being in a house full of vampires.

Then the two hunters walked in behind him. A tall man with enough muscle to put Marcus to shame and an Asian woman of almost the same height. Their eyes scanned the sitting room no doubt taking in every aspect of it to report back to the guild before landing on Piper.

"Tristan, Mizuki. You remember Piper, don't you?" Vincent gestured to the two hunters behind him and then to Angelica.

"Yes," Tristan said, his eyes narrowing on the fake Piper. "It's been a while. Some of us thought maybe you weren't coming back."

Mizuki said nothing. Her eyes laser points on the fake Piper.

Angelica must have found her backbone because she sat there with an air of confidence that wasn't there before. Perhaps it was only vampires that made her antsy. A lopsided grin appeared on her face. One that I'd seen on Piper's face many times before. Just seeing it made my heart clench tight.

"I didn't know you needed me badly. What did you do without me?" The snarky tone of her voice made Rayne and Wynn's heads jerk her way. Her portrayal was almost too good. I hesitated to see the reaction from Vincent.

Vincent threw his head back and laughed. "That's a good one, Ms. Billings."

"It's Durand." Fake Piper quipped back with a tight smile.

"Of course. Of course." He slicked his hand over his dark hair and tugged on one of the large diamond earrings glinting in his ears. "I could see how one would think that we are incapable of doing our job without you." He strode forward and stopped before her, not taking the available seat nearby. To my surprise, Angelica didn't react to his close threatening presence. "But I do want to assure you that we indeed do know how to do our job. Quite well as you do remember." His eyes skipped over to Rayne before slowly dragging his gaze back to Piper. "I would hate to have to provide you with a reminder of our capabilities."

Fake Piper lifted her chin and stared down at Vincent. "The only reminder I need is when you will be coming by again. Because frankly I need a full twenty-four hours' notice to prepare myself for the onslaught of your cologne." She wrinkled her nose and sneered.

Shit. Angelica. Too far. You are pushing him too far.

The two hunters stepped forward and Vincent held up a hand. "It's alright. I was unreasonable in showing up here so soon. I simply worried you might have forgotten your end of the deal." He turned slightly to grin at the rest of us, his teeth gnashing together so hard that I swore he'd have been a better vampire than human. "You will forgive me for my intrusion."

I inclined my head. "It is understandable. Unfortunately, we have nothing to report."

"As I told you on the phone, Vincent." Wynn jumped in with a lazy grin. "After the council exonerated Allister and killed Morpheus, they have been on the move. We haven't been able to pin them down in one place for longer than a day."

Vincent sighed. "Well, that is disappointing. I had hoped for better news. I would like nothing more than to get this over with so that we may all go back to our lives." He looked at Piper pointedly. "I will be checking in again soon. I hope to hear better news by then."

"Of course," I gestured toward the door with a gracious half bow. "Darren, would you be so kind as to escort our guests to their vehicle?"

"This way." Darren started out of the room. Except the two hunters didn't move. They stared at Piper for a long moment before shifting their gaze to Vincent.

Vincent waved a hand and started forward. "Let us leave. I have a stack of reports to go through and I want it to be done in time for the new episode of my show tonight."

Rayne's mouth twitched and I shot him a look. We didn't need a reason for the hunters to loiter longer on our premises. The fact that we were getting them out of here this easily was a gift from some higher being.

Soon the door to the house closed and Darren appeared back in the room with a strained frown. "They have left."

Angelica blew out a long breath and sagged in her chair. "About fucking time. I don't know how your girl does it. I couldn't handle facing vampires and those assholes all the time." Her southern twang became heavier with each word. "How many more times am I expected to deal with those kinds of people?"

"As many times as you are required," Darren reminded her with a scowl. "You signed a contract and have been paid. We expect you to do your part. Or we will contact your employer."

Angelica's or rather Piper's face went white. "No. No. I got this. No need to do anything drastic. I can handle a few jerk wads. Wouldn't be my first time."

"As for the incident with Rayne earlier," I began with a firm frown. "I do not want to hear of anything like that happening again. Just do your job or we will have to let you go. I would hate to have to blemish your perfect record."

Standing up, Angelica brushed her hands over the front of her pants. "I got you. Perfect angel from now on. Cross my heart and hope to die."

Rayne flashed his fangs at her maliciously. "Oh, you will. I can promise you that."

CHAPTER 10

Piper

MY LIPS TUGGED DOWN into a frown. I ran my hand over my stomach that had begun to swell more than before. I turned one way and then the other looking at the way my stomach protruded over my pants in the mirror.

I sighed and dropped my shirt. No matter how I look at it, no matter how many times I tell myself that it's just because I'm pregnant, my brain still sees that I'm getting fat. Even in a dream.

Turning from the mirror in my bedroom, my heart jumped into my throat. "Damn it, Antoine. Make a noise would you."

Antoine's lips twitched. He leaned against the bedroom door, his suit jacket and tie gone this time and his hands tucked into his pockets. His pale gaze slid over my form and settled on my stomach. I forced myself not to shy away from his gaze.

"You are lovely, Piper. Never doubt that."

I pouted and placed my hands on my stomach over my shirt. "I know. Just feeling self-conscious today, I guess."

"Why do you think that is?" Antoine asked, moving away from the door frame and walking with precise steps toward me.

I sank into his arms as he slid them around me, letting his hands settle on my hips. "I don't know. I'm probably being silly. It's just, I'm here and you are all at home and I just feel so..." My throat tightened. "...alone."

Antoine lifted his hand from my hip and stroked my hair away from my face. "I understand. However, without any idea of where you are we are unable to reach you. Have you been able to find anything out that could help Rayne search for you?"

I chewed on my lower lip and pinched my brows together as I thought. I hadn't been able to go outside so trying to see what it looked like from the outside was a no go. "Well, we know I'm still in the same time zone. So that narrows it down some..." I trailed off and then my eyes lit up. "I don't know what it looks like from the outside but I convinced them to let me walk around the courtyard. That's in the middle of the building or at least I think it is."

Antoine nodded. "I can have Rayne search for buildings with a courtyard. What does it look like?"

"Well..." I began picturing the courtyard in my head. "There are four floors. With windows pointing into the courtyard. The walls are made up of some kind of old-fashioned stone in an off white grayish color. There's a pretty fountain in the middle..."

"Do you remember what it looked like?"

I lifted my head to meet his gaze. "Will it help? Knowing what the fountain looks like I mean?"

Antoine cupped the side of my face and stroked his thumb over my cheek. "Anything right now could be the imperative to us finding you."

I blew out a breath and lifted my eyes up to the ceiling. "It was like marble or something. With a woman...I think? Yeah. It was definitely a woman 'cause I remember thinking her nipples were really pointy."

Antoine chuckled and pressed a kiss to my forehead. "Of course, you would."

My lips pursed and looked at him warily. "Why are you being so lovey dovey all of a sudden?"

Leaning away from me, Antoine tilted his head to one side. "What do you mean?"

"Well, if I didn't know it was impossible for anyone else to be in my dreams 'cause of the whole blood bond thing, then I would think that you'd been possessed by one of those body snatchers they talk about on those sci fi shows."

Antoine let out an impatient sigh and stepped away from me. "I can promise you I am who I have always been." He held his hands out to either side letting me look over his form, then he added on, "However..."

"Oh no." I sank down on the nearby chair. "Here we go. Just give me the bad news already. I can take it."

Shaking his head, Antoine moved a few steps closer until he stood before me. I braced myself for whatever he had to say. If Antoine was worried then the rest of the guys were probably freaking the fuck out and that just made me want to freak the fuck out.

"Vincent stopped by."

Just those three words made me want to throw up. I knew Vincent would come by sometime. I knew it was just dumb luck that he hadn't until now. All kinds of scenarios began to swirl around in my head and even in a dream my heartbeat ratcheted up until it was throbbing in my throat.

I gripped the edges of the bed and licked my lips. "And what happened with Vincent?"

Antoine's gaze focused on me in a way that I hadn't seen since I learned that they were vampires.

"Fucking hell, Antoine. Just spit it out already. The anticipation is killing me. Where did you tell him I was?"

"Vincent knew where you were."

My face pinched together in confusion. "What? He knows where I am? How did he figure that out and can he tell me?"

"Because you were there."

I shot up from the bed and waved my hands in front of me. "Hold up. How was I there? I'm here."

Pursing his lips, Antoine stroked his thumb and forefinger over his bottom lip. "We have hired a witch to take your place."

I gaped, my eyes suddenly burning with tears. "I just told you how I was feeling insecure about me being here and you guys were all over there and now you're telling me that you hired a witch to replace me?" I stomped up to him and shoved a finger at his chest. "You are one sick bastard. It doesn't matter who it is, does it? You just want someone to sink your fangs into, anyone would do!" I smacked his chest with my fist. "Here I am worried sick about you all and missing you like some kind of sap when you're off getting your jollies off with Piper 2.0. Tell me. Is she prettier than me? Huh? Huh?"

Antoine kept quiet while I ranted, not even flinching at my blows.

"Are you going to say something or not you asshole?" I growled, wishing I had my own fangs to rip into him.

Antoine watched me with calm eyes. "Are you quite finished?"

I breathed heavily, sucking in more and more breath until I felt like I might pass out. "Not even close."

"Then please...by all means...let me have it." Antoine gestured toward me with a hand and then added on, "Actually, hold on a moment." He walked over to the chair I'd been on and sat down, crossing one leg over the other. "Proceed."

I stared at him with open horror, then clipped my mouth shut and turned my back on him. "Fuck you, Antoine. Just leave me alone."

Silence drifted between us for a long moment and I thought perhaps he had actually left until he spoke again.

"We hired a witch to glamour herself as you to trick Vincent and the other hunters. In no way is she a replacement for you." He continued talking to my back. "In fact, just the other day Rayne was two seconds away from killing her for daring to pretend to be you in a more personal fashion."

Antoine paused, letting me take it all in.

"You think you're alone in this," Antoine's presence filled in behind me, his fingers curling over my shoulders. My back stiffened at his touch. "You're not. The pain and loneliness you feel. I feel it as well."

"Only because you have to," I bit out bitterly.

Antoine squeezed my shoulders lightly. "Even more so because I know how you feel. It rips me apart to know you are in pain and I am not able to be here to help you. If you think you are suffering alone in this then you do not know us at all. We suffer as you suffer. Perhaps even more so since we are unable to be there to protect our offspring."

I snorted and turned around in his arms. "You call that an apology? Who told you to say that, Darren?"

An emotion flickered over Antoine's face for a brief second before it was gone but I saw it.

"What? What is it?" I smacked him on the chest with my palm. "What's going on with Darren?"

"It is nothing to worry about." He brushed his fingers through my hair and kissed my forehead. "I should go. You need your sleep. I'll get the information you gave me to Rayne."

"Now, hold up a second." I grabbed for him. "You can't just leave me hanging like that. What's going on with Darren?"

"Good night." He disappeared before I could get another word out.

"Fucking hell." I threw my hands up in the air with a scowl. "I'm missing all the good stuff." I glanced at myself in the mirror once more and frowned. "Baby, trust me when I say this fucking sucks."

CHAPTER 11

Marcus

"AND YOU'RE SURE THAT'S where Piper is?" Drake asked, peering over Rayne's shoulder at the computer screen.

I stood to the side, trying but failing to not look as anxious as I felt.

Rayne sighed and typed harder on the computer keyboard. "For the last time, yes, I'm sure. There are only five buildings with the same kind of courtyard Piper described and the same type of design that the council has previously shown to be interested in."

"So?" Drake leaned against the desk and chair, making Rayne visible tense. "How do you know which of those five Piper's is in?"

Stopping mid-type, Rayne shoved his chair so that Drake stumbled back from him with a glare. "Look, do you want to do this?"

Drake growled, crossing his arms over his chest. "I would if I had the patience to sit there and stare at a screen all day."

Snorting, Rayne turned back to the computer and started typing again. "But you can watch hours of football without any trouble."

Smacking Rayne on the back of the head, Drake said, "That's different."

My patience broke.

"Will you stop your squabbling? You're worse than children. Piper is alone, pregnant, and in enemy territory. And here you are arguing over football."

Rayne and Drake stared at me for a long moment before turning back to each other.

"Football is entertaining," Drake continued as if I hadn't spoken. "Staring at words on a screen for hours on end is mind numbingly dull."

"To you, maybe," Rayne quipped. "To me, it's stimulating. Besides, without me, you wouldn't have any idea where Piper is."

Drake threw his hands up in the air. "I still don't know where she is!"

"She's right..." Rayne zoomed in on the screen until a topside view of the supposed building Piper was being held appeared. "Here."

"But how do you know?" Drake dragged out with a huff of frustration.

"Because, I know."

"And I'm just supposed to take your word for it."

I rubbed my forehead, a headache beginning to form.

This was pointless.

"What's the address?" I interjected, unable to handle their chattering any longer.

Rayne stopped and glanced up at me with a wary frown. "Why?"

"Because I'm going to get her back," I replied, figuring the answer was obvious.

Drake and Rayne exchanged a look. Then Drake pointed out, "You can't do that."

I snarled, flashing my fangs at him. "Why not? We know where she is. Let's get her back."

Rayne shook his head. "As much as we would like to go busting down the door, fangs blazing. We don't know where they are keeping Piper in the building or how many we would be up against. Then there is the fact that they could turn around and use Piper as a hostage. They could very well decide to kill her the moment we stepped on the property."

"Then what?" I threw my hands up violently. "You suggest we do nothing?"

"I didn't say that," Rayne closed his computer top with a snap of the lid. "What I'm saying is that we should be smart about this. We need to make initial contact, let the council know that we know where she is."

"And how do we go about doing that?" Allister asked, walking into the room behind us and stopped next to his brother.

"Well..." Rayne leaned back in his chair far more calmly about the situation that I felt. I hadn't felt this riled up since I had to put down my sword at the battle of Tripoli.

"There are many ways we could play this. We could send a letter to Tuma and the others requesting an audience. We could simply do that whole, we know where you are bit," Rayne chuckled, smirking. "Always a classic."

"Why don't we just send a note to Piper? Leave the council out of it all together?" Drake pointed out with a proud grin. "Then she knows we are coming for her."

"But how do you know they'll even give her the note?" Allister added on. "They could take the note and just throw it away and then Piper wouldn't know anything."

"Antoine could just tell her in one of their dream meetups," Drake shrugged in return. "No need to send anything."

Rayne waved a hand in front of him. "No. That wouldn't work. We still want the council to know we know where she is and that we aren't just going to sit around and let them fuck us over."

"Hmmm." The three of them went quiet for a moment.

They all had fair points. I still preferred my option of running in there and just taking Piper back. However, I could see how that could be dangerous for Piper in the long run. God do I miss the days where everything was far more formal. If you kept someone as a hostage, you'd set up a meeting, negotiate the return of said hostage and then run the other one through. Now, everything had to be delicately handled. Things were easier when you could just talk with your fists.

"Maybe we should ask Antoine what he thinks?" Allister finally offered up. "He might have some more insight into the council that we do not. Some kind of idea as to what we should do to get their attention and yet still make sure that Piper gets the note or whatever."

"Good idea," Rayne wagged his finger in the air and then without warning yelled, "Antoine! Come down here."

The three of us winced against the volume of Rayne's voice.

"Fuck, Rayne," Drake growled, wiggling a finger in his ear. "Couldn't you have just gone up there or something. Way to break our fucking ear drums."

Rayne rolled his eyes. "You'll heal."

A few moments later, footsteps sounded on the stairs. Antoine appeared at the bottom of the stairs with Wynn and Darren in tow.

"Yes?" Antoine arched a brow at the four of us. "I can only assume you have called me down here like a dog because you have something of importance to tell us?"

"Rayne figured out where Piper is being held," Drake said without warning. "We are trying to decide on a plan of action."

"I think we should send her a note of some kind," Rayne offered up, glancing around the room from his chair. "Something that lets her know we are coming for her but also tells the council that we know where she is and we aren't going to take their shit anymore."

"This is ridiculous," I snapped, tired of all of their calm expressions. "We should be breaching their walls and taking back what is ours. Not sitting here discussing it amongst ourselves. Right now Piper could be endangered and none of us can do anything about it."

Antoine placed a hand on my shoulder. "I understand your frustration, my friend. We all want Piper back sooner rather than later. However.." Antoine let his gaze drift over the others. "We cannot be rash in how we decide this. Piper's very life may depend on it."

"That's what I said," Rayne shot me a smug look.

"I also," Antoine continued without removing his hand from me. "Do not think a simple note will suffice. We must make a statement of sorts."

Wynn stepped into the conversation. "How do you propose that? We can't very well send a smoke signal telling them to let her go or else."

Antoine inclined his head. "Yes, it must be a subtle thing. Something that cannot be interpreted as anything other than a concern for Piper's wellbeing. If the council believes we are threatening them they will move her and then we may never figure out where she is again."

"Then what do we do?" Drake leaned back against the wall and stared hard at the ground. "If we send a note then they will just throw it away. If they don't misinterpret what we say in the note. It could be taken in so many ways we don't mean."

"Precisely," Antoine agreed, dropping his hand from my shoulder. "So, we won't send a note. Or a letter."

I startled and glared, "But we have to do something. I will not sit by while they make fools out of us."

"I do not think any of you mean to let that happen either, Marcus." Antoine locked his gaze with mine. "We are going to send Piper a package. And inside will be something from each of us. Something that reminds her that we are thinking of her and care about her."

"Won't they just throw that away too?" Allister asked what we were all thinking.

Antoine adjusted the cuffs of his shirt. "No. Tuma is far too sentimental to allow such a thing. He will have it searched no doubt so it cannot be something so obvious as we are coming for you." Antoine peered into each of our eyes in turn, making sure that the weight of his gaze was felt. "So, take some time to think of what you would like to send. All items must be approved. We cannot mess this up."

CHAPTER 12

Piper

"SPECIAL DELIVERY!" TUMA WALKED into my room with a package in his hands.

I looked up from my book and blinked at the vampire. "What's this?"

Tuma held the box out to me with a grin. "It seems your men were so concerned about you that they hunted down our location. Thankfully, they did not do anything rash and put your life at risk by coming here. Instead..." he nodded at the box. "They sent this."

I took the box from him slowly, my heart rate picking up at the very thought of what could be inside of it. I knew the guys would find me once I told Antoine the description of the courtyard. The council might think they are good but my guys are better.

Tuma stared down at me with a forced grin on his face. "Well...aren't you going to open it?"

Glancing down at the box and then back up at Tuma, I wrinkled my nose with a skeptical look. "I'm not sure that's a good idea."

Cocking his head to the side, Tuma glanced from the box to me. "Why not? I should see what is inside to make sure it is not some ruse."

Tapping the box with my finger, I pointed out, "Shouldn't you have done that before bringing it to me? If you were really worried about my safety, I would think that all packages would need to be checked before being brought anywhere near me."

Tuma tapped his stick on the ground three times. "Do not think I am neglecting your safety, Miss Durand. My security team ran it through one of those x-ray machines they use at the airport. They did not see anything that could be considered harmful. However..." he sat down next to me on the couch. "I would be remiss if I did not see what your men thought was so important to send you that they could not wait until they saw you again."

Seeing that there was no way out of this one, I turned my attention back to the package. "I need some scissors."

Tuma produced a knife.

It appeared so suddenly beside my face, that I gasped and grabbed my chest. "Fucking hell. Don't do that. You know I'm pregnant right? I could have had a freaking heart attack."

"My apologies." Tuma handed me the knife handle first. "Please, do carry on."

Grasping the knife in my hand, I slit the box open. I hesitated from returning the knife to Tuma. For a brief second, the urge to stab him through the neck with the sharp point was almost too much to ignore.

I couldn't.

As much as it would have brought me immense pleasure to knock that smug look off of his smiling face, killing Tuma wouldn't do me any good. I would still have to figure out how to get out of this place on my own. I had no idea how to get to the front door, only the courtyard and for all I know there were half a dozen rooms between there and the exit.

And what would I do once I got free? Where would I go? I had no phone, no id, no money. I had no way to get back home. They would find me and catch me within an hour. Maybe more if someone found Tuma's body sooner.

With a reluctant sigh, I handed the knife back to Tuma and focused on the box in my hands. Opening the flaps, I braced myself for what the guys could have sent me. I frowned at the contents. Confusion furrowed my brow.

It was a bunch of random knickknacks.

I picked up a pen and examined it. It was one of Antoine's. Only he would have something so expensive as a pen. The others didn't care about writing utensils the way that he did. They didn't have to do mounds of paperwork every day either. Giving me one of his pens was a serious thing. It was like giving me one of his kidneys. My eyes pricked with emotion.

Setting the pen to the side, I picked up a small foam basketball with a sticky note attached to it. 'Squeeze me.' Not sure if I should do it in front of Tuma, but too curious to resist, I squeezed the little orange ball. It started to vibrate in my hand. Confused, I squeezed it again to make it stop. Then I noticed something written in black marker on the side of it. This said, 'Piper's button relaxer.'

Huh? What in the world... My eyes widened and my face heated. I quickly placed the ball to the side and internally reminded myself to kick Drake's butt for embarrassing me.

The next thing was a book. Flipping open the inside cover, there was an inscription.

To help you sleep at night. — A

"Her Cross To Bear?" Tuma read over my shoulder. "What an odd name for a book. What is it about?"

I placed the book to the side and muttered, "Vampires, romance and stuff."

I wasn't about to tell him it was basically a book all about killing vampires and other supernatural beings while the female lead fucked the very beings she was supposed to be fighting. I didn't think that would endear me to Tuma much.

Allister had a weird sense of humor.

Setting the book aside, I reached into the box and pulled out the next item. This one was a little square mirror. I held it up and looked into it. What the heck? My finger must have hit something because the mirror screen changed to an image of Rayne and me cuddling on the couch a few months ago. My eyes burned and I quickly put the picture away.

Wynn's gift was the most obvious and probably the most embarrassing. A pair of silk underwear that I knew I'd seen him wear on more than one occasion. He was so full of himself. Like I needed a pair of his underwear to remember him by. Still, I tucked the silk fabric underneath one of my legs and tried to control my raging hormones.

I wasn't sure what Marcus would send me. He wasn't exactly the gift type. Marcus was more of the spending time with you, watching you do your work, and then railing you into the mattress type. Just thinking about it was getting me all worked up. Not that it was hard nowadays.

Being pregnant was not all fun and babies. Half the time I was crying and then the other half, I was hornier than a rabbit in mating season. Several times I'd woken up orgasming just from some dream I had. It was really embarrassing and a bit annoying. Because when I woke up, I was even more hot and bothered and then there was no one there to help me out with it. I certainly wasn't going to ask Tuma or Agnes to help me out with something. I'd rather die.

Thankfully, all that Marcus sent me was a red bouncy ball. Those kinds that you spend fifty cents on and get out of a crank machine at restaurants. I wasn't sure about the symbolism in that but figured he was trying to help me from being bored.

The last thing in the box had to be from Darren. This was a plain piece of paper with eight words on it.

Remember that day on the beach in Seabrick?

Yeah. I did remember that day.

Darren and I had been hiding from the hunter's guild for a while by then and we had just started to see each other in a different light. I'd just had a shitty day at work and was frustrated by the lack of communications from the others when Darren surprised me with a picnic on the beach.

It was so beautiful that day. The sun was setting and the waves were gently crashing on the shore. It was off season so there weren't that many people on the beach. Darren and I sat there eating and laughing and just talking about nothing. Then he took me home and made love to me until we both passed out in each other's arms.

Out of all the days in hiding, that was one of the best nights of my life.

I carefully folded the note and sniffed, placing it back in the box and started to put back the others. "Uh...thanks Tuma. These are really great. They helped me so much."

Tuma watched me carefully as if he couldn't quite figure me out. "You really do love them, don't you?"

I blinked at him, swiping at the tears on my face. "Why do you ask that?"

Tuma shook his head and stood. "I just realized that until now I didn't really believe you loved them all the way you said you did. But seeing your face as you picked up each item, it made me realize that maybe we aren't the monsters we think we are after all."

I peered up at him. "You don't have to be. It's a choice. One that the Durands have done very well with."

Tuma bobbed his head and walked to the door. He paused in the doorway. "I will consider letting one of your men visit you. Only one. Decide which one it will be and let me know."

CHAPTER 13

Piper

HOW THE HELL WAS I supposed to pick just one of them to come visit me?

That was like asking me to pick a favorite star in the sky. A favorite donut out of the donut holes. Fucking impossible.

On the subject of donuts, I could really go for something sweet right now. Oooo and some cheese. I would kill for a block of cheddar cheese.

I looked up from the book I was pretending to read to where Agnes stared at the television. The woman had a serious problem. From the moment they put it in my room, she has spent every moment she could watching it.

We burned over the pregnancy related videos pretty quickly and now she is deep into season four of some comedy about a bunch of scientists. I didn't get it. I liked my television with a bit more drama and a whole lot more sex.

I shifted in my seat, a sudden urge to find that toy Drake sent came over me. I just hoped that Agnes was too absorbed in her show to notice my arousal. Though, the fact that it was basically my constant state of being nowadays I would think she was used to it.

If I wasn't so horny, I was seriously looking at Tuma in a different light, then I was crying from not being able to find my favorite shoes. Then there was the fact that every single piece of clothing I had made my nipples ache and I wanted nothing more than to lay around naked but noooo I couldn't do that here.

I just wanted to go home.

"You seem distressed," Agnes shifted her gaze away from the television albeit reluctantly.

I flicked my eyes up at her. "You think?"

Agnes picked the controller up and paused the show. "Would you like to talk about it?"

I picked up my cup of herbal tea, an atrocious invention but better than nothing and asked, "Uh...with you?"

Shrugging, Agnes shifted in her seat and turned to me, her hands in her lap. "We have no one else to talk to. I am bound by my blood bond to Tuma to serve as he instructs and he commands I take care of you. I would assume that means not only physically but emotionally. And since I cannot do anything as of yet about your current condition," she gestured to my growing stomach. "I can at least try and help you with your emotional one. Unless you would like me to help you relieve your rising libido?"

Choking on my tea, I coughed for several moments earning me a hard pat on the back from Agnes. I waved her off and sat my tea down. "What now?"

Agnes moved back to her seat and calmly explained, "Well, as I understand it, about this time in your progression your libido will be on the rise and seeing as none of your lovers are available you must be...how do I put this?" she hummed and then flashed her fangs at me. "Going batshit crazy?"

I snorted and then after a moment threw my head back and laughed. I laughed so hard that I ended up going into another coughing fit. Chuckling, I shook my head. "Yeah. I guess so. But I think I'm good, thanks anyway."

"Very well," Agnes pursed her lips and then cocked her head to the side. "Besides your raging libido what else can I help you with?"

Dragging my foot up under me, I looked at Agnes. "Look, I appreciate your offer to help but I don't really think this is something you can help me with."

Arching a brow, Agnes retorted, "I've been alive for several hundred years. There is nothing you can say that I will be surprised by."

I sighed and gave up. "Fine. Tuma said I could have one of the guys come to visit and he wants me to choose one of them to come."

"And..."

"And I don't know which one to choose. How can I choose?" I sank down into the couch and groaned. "It's like freaking choosing between...between..." I grunted and lamely finished, "...between one hard thing and another."

"I see."

Agnes didn't say anything for a long moment and then proposed something to me that I hadn't thought of.

"Which one at this point in time would help you with your current condition?" She eyed my belly pointedly.

Rubbing a hand over my belly, I pressed my lips together firmly. "Well...I don't know. It's hard to imagine any of them with a baby. I mean, none of the vampires put it there."

"I understand." Agnes nodded. "It is near impossible that any of the vampires were able to impregnate you. It is most likely the offspring of the human servant."

"Uh...yeah. What you said."

"Then the choice should be easy," Agnes said with such confidence that I envied her.

"I don't follow."

Agnes stood from the couch and picked up my tea cup, moving around the room cleaning up other things as she went. "It is quite obvious you should invite the father of the child to visit you. He is the only one who could possibly connect with you in the position you are in right now."

"Why do you think that is?" I turned in my seat, following her with my head around the room.

Pausing with her hands full of dishes and dirty laundry, Agnes locked eyes with me. "Because you're both human."

"I don't see how that's relevant." I shook my head and grabbed the discarded remote. "Just because we're both humans doesn't mean I should pick Darren. If anything, it's a reason not to pick him. He would be far more fragile than the others when faced with the council members."

"Yes, but..." Agnes paused behind the couch and placed a hand on my shoulder. "He is the only one you cannot interact with by drinking their blood."

I jerked around just in time to see her wink at me before she sauntered out of the room.

Well, that was an interesting suggestion. Especially coming from Agnes. I'd thought she was firmly on the council's side but it seems that the more time she spent with me the more she was softening toward me.

A month ago, Agnes wouldn't spend more than ten minutes in the room with me. Enough time to find out if I needed anything, to check the condition of my child, and then she was out the door.

Now, she was sitting with me for most of the day and even offering me advice on how to get around Tuma's orders.

I sank into the couch once more and grinned to myself. Well, son of a bitch. That woman — grumpy she may be — was a freaking genius.

I didn't have to pick between any of them. If I chose Darren, then he could bring me the blood of the other guys and then I could see all of them. I mean, it wasn't perfect. I wouldn't be seeing them in person but it was better than nothing.

Now the problem was figuring out how to make sure that Darren brought the blood with him...I glanced over at the bed and arched a brow. Well, I guess I could just tell Antoine in a dream.

I sighed and stood from the couch. It just seemed too simple. Something was bound to get screwed up. I wasn't that lucky.

I shot a look at the clock and frowned. I couldn't go to bed now. Antoine wasn't going to be sleeping anytime soon.

Well, what was I going to do? I had several hours to waste and all this anxious energy was only going to get worse the longer I waited around for it to be bedtime.

Catching sight of the orange basketball, Drake sent me my lips curled into a grin. Well, there was something I could take care of in the meantime. I practically skipped to the bedroom door and locked it.

I might like Agnes more than before but I still didn't want her to walk in on me fiddling my diddle. Especially not after her recent offer of helping me out. I grimaced and shoved that thought away. That was not going to get me in the mood. Though, honestly, the thought of sliced bread got me horny so Agnes wouldn't be too much of a stretch.

Now…if you put Drake on a piece of bread or rather Allister and Drake as the bread and I could be the in between of that sandwich. Hmmm what about the condiments? Who would be the mayo? Rayne would obviously be the ketchup. Wynn would be the cheese cause he was smooth like cheddar and then Marcus would be the pickle cause of that crunchy exterior with a soft interior.

Was I really comparing the guys to food products while getting ready to pleasure myself?

God, I hated being pregnant.

Now…where was that little ball…

CHAPTER 14

Darren

SITTING IN THE BACK of the limo instead of driving it was awkward. I much preferred the privacy the separator provided by sitting in the front seat. However, the council sent a limo for me and by what Antoine says I couldn't say no.

They wouldn't even let me bring anyone else with me. Which to me seemed suspicious but Antoine once again reassured me that I would be safe. Tuma was a vampire of his word and he would not think to relieve him of his only other human servant.

As if that was such a tragedy.

Things with Antoine had been tense since my outburst. I could not seem to let myself be happy or feel even an iota of pleasure with Piper so far away from us. I didn't know if it was because of the pregnancy or…actually I knew it was.

Piper was a strong and capable woman. She had proven herself many times over. Even so much so to take on the hunter's guild on her own. When comparing her to any of the vampires, I would bet on her every time.

It's just the thought of my offspring inside of her and not being able to be there for her. For her to be in the hands of the enemy, while all we could do was sit around and wait made my inside twist and snarl together.

There was nothing I could do to ease this sickening feeling inside of me.

My hands tensed around the box in my hand as the vials clinked together. I didn't have much confidence that I would be allowed to bring the item inside with me. Once more I was relying on Antoine's experience and he thought that Tuma wouldn't care about the blood. I didn't think so.

Why would the vampire allow me to bring the blood of the other vampires into their home? They barely wanted me to come visit Piper. To give her more access to her vampires would not be prudent on their part.

The limo pulled into a gravel driveway, causing the wheels to crackle with each inch we progressed toward the prison. To call the place they were keeping Piper anything other than that was being naïve. They were keeping her prisoner and that was all there was to it. Anyone who thought differently was fooling themselves.

We stopped briefly at the gate before after an exchange of words from the driver we moved into the interior of the gates. I tried to look uninterested as we drove by but my eyes took in everything in the dim twilight.

Visiting Piper wasn't the only reason for my coming. I'd been instructed in length from Marcus, Drake, and Allister on what to look for and how to remember it without writing it down. Six guards in the front, six members of the house of Durand. I didn't need to take note of the building's exterior, Rayne assured us that he could see that from some satellite system. The outside they could handle. I needed to let them know what they were up against.

Two guards at the door, like the two most important people in my life.

"Here we are," the driver announced before the door opened for me.

I held the box under my arm and slid out of the vehicle. One of the guards approached me, his hard eyes moving over my form. I'd kept on my suit and gloves, choosing to look non-threatening by blending in with the staff. In my experience, the vampires — even the guards — paid less attention to servants than to those dressed in street clothes. I wasn't sure what that said about them but I was thankful for it now.

The guard jerked his head, instructing me to follow him.

Keeping a good pace behind him, I allowed my eyes to wander. The inside was not much different than my own home except it seemed that the council preferred more modern style than of the old world Boris had enjoyed.

My gaze trailed down to the white tile floors. They must be a bitch to remove blood from. Though, I supposed they didn't really care who saw what they did here...

"Stop."

Another two guards stood before the interior door, leading into I had no idea. They did not care for the open floor plan that most modern homes did. Marcus will be overjoyed by that. Having an open floor plan would have made it more difficult to sneak about. Nowhere to take cover as he'd say.

"What's that?" The guard who had stopped us pointed to the box in my hands.

I held the box up for them. "A gift for Piper."

The guard moved closer, eyeing the box warily. "What's in it?"

Rather than trying to fool them, I told them the truth. "Blood of my masters for the baby."

The guards exchanged a look before the first one asked his partner. "Is that allowed?"

His partner shrugged. "I don't know. It's not a weapon. Should we ask the masters?"

The first one shook his head. "No. They're feeding. I don't want to be the one to interrupt them. Do you?"

The second guard paled and shook his head vigorously. "No. I'm good."

I took in their exchange with a bored expression, something I had grown proficient at in the service of the Durands. The more worried I looked, the more likely they would think something was going on. I couldn't let them think that.

"Can I go?" I asked, keeping my voice neutral.

The guards looked at each other once more and then nodded. "Fine. You can take it with you but don't make trouble. We don't want to pay for it."

"Understood." I inclined my head as one servant to another.

The guard I entered with ushered me through the doorway and to the left. Two doors, one left, four guards, then six guards. I could only imagine how many guards they had during the day if they had so many watching them when they were awake.

"It's just down here," my guide instructed me.

We passed a few servants and a few humans with bite marks on their neck. The servants didn't even blink twice at me and the ones with bites only gave me a curious look before lowering their gaze and skittering away.

How many humans did they employ here? Were all of them here of their own volitions or were some of them bought and paid for?

It was something to think about later. Right now, I had to focus on the task at hand.

Four doors and then a right. Two doors and then...

"Right here." The guard stopped before the door and then lifted his hand and knocked briefly.

To my surprise, he didn't stay.

The door opened a moment later and an older woman in a peasant dress that was more like those of when before I came to work for Antoine. Her eyes shot to my face and a look of relief came over it.

"Thank the maker," the woman cried out and grabbed me by the arm and jerked me into the room. "Maybe you can get her to calm down."

"I told you to get out of here, Agnes," Piper's voice screeched out of what I could only assume was the bathroom followed by the sound of several things breaking.

I restrained myself from rushing to Piper's side. "What's going on?"

Agnes grimaced and then gave me a clearly forced smile. "Oh, you know. Second trimester woes and all that. She will be delighted to see you though."

We stopped before the door and Agnes didn't bother knocking before pushing the door open. "Piper, look who has come to see you!"

Littered in broken glass and towels, you could barely see the bathroom floor or what there was of it. Then there was Piper sitting in the middle of the floor in a bathrobe, her face blotchy, both hands clutching handfuls of tissues.

"Darren?" Piper asked through blurry eyes and then screamed and threw the tissue box at me. It hit me in the chest with a soft thud. "You did this to me. Look at me? I'm a disgusting mess."

"I can see…" I let my eyes trail over the disaster she had created in the bathroom. "I have to say I'm a little disappointed."

"I'll just let you two get reacquainted." Agnes patted me on the arm and ducked out of the room.

"Disappointed?" Piper gaped at me. "Disappointed? I have spent the last…" she counted on her fingers and then growled, "fucking who knows how long here without any of you to help me while I grow *your* child," she pointed a shaky finger at me.

Arching a brow, I sat the box on the counter nearby. Then calmly approached her.

"No. No. Go away." She waved me off and scooched across the floor. "I don't want to see you."

"Oh?" I questioned, kneeling at her side. "So, I should leave?"

"No!" she practically launched herself at me, her nails biting into my arm. "Don't you dare leave. I can't do this without you." She shook her head, and leaned against me, her shoulders shaking through her sobs. "You don't know what it's like here. I'd rather be fighting rogue vampires than deal with these sociopaths. And this," she gestured down at her swelling stomach. "This thing hates me. I can feel it."

My lips ticked up on one side. "I highly doubt that."

"How would you know?" Piper glared at me before waddling to her feet. The sight would have made me chuckle had she not already been in a mood. "You don't have a demon spawn growing inside of you."

I stayed on the ground where I was watching as she slowly made her way to the sink. "Is that how you really feel? That it's some kind of demonic creature?"

"What?" Piper turned on the water. "Of course not. Aren't you listening to me? This thing." She pulled a washcloth into the sink. "Is trying to kill me! I can't sleep. I want the weirdest ass things. I asked for an olive and peanut butter sandwich today!" She wrung the washcloth out and exclaimed, "I hate olives!"

This time I couldn't help but let out a small chuckle.

Piper whirled around. "Are you laughing at me?"

I moved to my feet and approached her with my hands out in front of me. "No, never. I'm just so happy to see you."

Piper let me wrap my arms around her. She placed her head on my shoulder and sank into my arms with a sigh. "I'm just so tired."

"I understand," I murmured, brushing my hands over her hair and down her back. "We are working on getting you out."

Piper lifted her head from my shoulder and locked eyes with me. "Why can't you take me with you when you leave?"

Sliding my thumb beneath one eye and then the other, I caught her welling tears. "You know I can't do that. Not yet."

"Ugh," Piper exclaimed and opened her mouth no doubt to give me an earful before she stopped. Her eyes zeroed in on my hands. "Why are you wearing your gloves?"

"Oh," I dropped my hands, lacing them behind my back. "No reason. Let's go to the other room. I brought you something."

"No, you don't." Piper grabbed me by the lapels of my suit jacket and shoved me against the counter. "You don't get to come in here and order me around. I want to know what's going on with your hands."

I slicked my hand through my black hair. "It's nothing. Please do not worry."

"Fine." Piper crossed her arms over her chest and stared me down. "Then take them off."

Locking eyes with her, I contemplated how I was going to get out of this one. Seeing that pushing her was probably not a good idea right now in her state, I conceded. "Fine. I will."

"Good." Piper jerked her head at me. "I'm waiting."

Slowly, I lifted my hands before me and pulled on the middle finger of the first glove. Jerking each finger in turn, I slipped the glove off and tucked it into my pocket. Then I proceeded to do the other one. Each finger that came out of the material felt like a piece of my heart being exposed.

"Happy?" I asked with a forced smile, showing her my bare hands.

"Not hardly." Piper pushed on my shoulders with her hands. "Get on your knees."

Taken a back, I blinked at her. "What?"

"You heard me. On your knees." She pointed down to the ground with a straight face.

Arching a brow, I slowly lowered to the ground. "Since when did you become the dominant one in this relationship?"

Piper smirked and cupped my chin up. "Oh, baby. I've always been in charge, you were just too busy getting your dick wet to notice."

CHAPTER 15

Piper

SEEING DARREN ON HIS knees was a kink I didn't know I had until he was kneeling before me. Commanding him to get on the floor was a random thought that came out of my mouth before I knew what I was doing. Then once he did it, I just had to go with it.

Now that I had him, I had to figure out what to do with him.

Shifting from one foot to the other, I turned to the counter and leaned against the edge, sliding myself up onto it. Or tried to, nothing was easy with the majority of my body mass forcing me forward.

"Here…let me help…" Darren moved to get off his knees.

"No!" I glared at him, shifting myself inch by inch onto the counter. "I got this. I've had this for the last five months. I don't need you to help me now."

Darren's lips turned down. "Piper."

"Stop it." I shot another glower his way. "I don't want your pity."

Blowing out a slow breath, Darren edged closer to me, his face in line with my knees. Sliding his hands up the outside of my thighs, pushing my robe to the side, his lips pressed softly against one knee and then the other.

"Darren," I groaned, the sexy mood slipping away from me. "I'm not in the mood anymore."

Darren peered up at me from my lap and murmured, "Then talk to me."

I rolled my neck and stared up at the ceiling, Darren's hands massaging down my legs and over my ankles. "I don't know what to say. We both know what I've been doing. Sitting around, miserable, and alone. While you all fuck around with a fake version of me."

"No one is fucking around with Angelica."

"Oh, it has a name?" I growled, the sudden urge to kick him in the face coming up quickly.

"Yes, she does. Her name is Angelica, she works at the Your Wish Club." Darren's fingers wrapped around my bare foot, pressing into the balls of my feet. A gasp and then low moan escaped me, my mind far away from their betrayal.

"Uh-huh. Sounds like a strip club," I murmured, my head lulling back.

Darren's finger didn't stop as he answered, "It is a strip club."

My head jerked up and I shoved my hips forward, dislodging his hands from my feet. My feet protested but my head overcame it. "You got this witch from a strip club?"

Pushing to his feet, too calm for my tastes, Darren brushed his knees off and leveled a look at me. "I did not get her from a strip club. She works at a strip club. I know her from the farmers market."

I blinked at him. "Huh?"

Darren shook his head and placed one hand on my hip and then the other. "Look, we had a problem and I approached Angelica about the issue and she agreed to pretend to be you until we could figure out a different solution."

Lower lip pushing out, I gripped his biceps slightly. "And what else was she doing while acting like me?"

Inching closer, Darren rubbed a hand up my back. "Cleaning, walking around, almost getting her head ripped off by Rayne."

"Really?" I smiled. "I mean, Antoine mentioned something but I didn't think he was serious."

Darren smiled back, leaning his forehead against mine. "I wasn't there but I heard about it from Angelica later. There was some misunderstanding and she almost pissed herself when he came at her with his fangs out."

"Hmmm," I lifted my arms and wrapped them around his neck, my libido ramping back up just at the thought of Rayne attacking some stripper for me. I curled my fingers into the nape of Darren's hair, tugging on it slightly. "And did she fool Vincent?"

Brushing his lips along my jaw and then burying his face in my neck, Darren hummed, his fingers finding their way to the front of my robe. "Yes, though he was more interested in finding out about the vampire council than caring about your strange behavior. Though, your two hunter friends seemed a bit more suspicious."

"Hunter friends?" I leaned back and looked at him.

Darren's gaze stayed down while he untied my robe. "You know that tall woman with scary eyes and the big guy with no hair and smiles too much."

"Oh," I bobbed my head in understanding, letting my robe drop to the ground. "Yeah, I guess Mizuki is a bit scary. And Tristan is just a big teddy bear. In fact, I think he and Marcus would get along great together." Darren cocked a brow. "I mean, if he wasn't a hunter and Marcus wasn't a vampire."

Darren huffed a laugh and then lifted me up by the back of my thighs as if I weighed nothing. "Now, where were we?"

I nipped at his lower lip and murmured, "I believe you were on your knees."

Sitting me on the counter once more, Darren cupped the back of my neck and kissed me until my toes curled. His tongue languished as it searched every crevice of my mouth while I gripped at his shoulders, trying to bring him closer to me. My blood raged in my ears and all of it was heading straight down between my thighs.

Jerking back from our kiss, I breathed heavily. "Down, now."

Darren smirked. "As you command." He lowered down to his knees, pressing kisses along the exposed flesh on the way. He lingered over my stomach taking a moment to caress and murmur to the bump before finally moving down to my spread thighs.

I angled back on my hands, my knees drawn up slightly to expose my aching heat to him.

The first touch of his breath on me made my back arch. I cried out, almost crying from the pleasure of it. How could I have gone this long without being touched by one of them?

"If possible, you taste even sweeter than before," Darren announced, his tongue sliding up the line of my folds. The tip circled around my clit and without warning my breath caught and a shuddery orgasm spread through me.

Darren pulled back from me with a curious frown. "Did you just?"

"Yes," I gasped, grabbing at him. "Now hurry up and fuck me."

"Why don't we move to the bedroom?" Darren offered, moving to his feet.

"No," I snarled, my fingers working on his pants. "I want you here and now. No waiting. I've waited long enough." I grasped his hot hard length in my hand, taking a moment to enjoy the feel of it. I didn't know how long he would be here and when I would get this chance again. I wanted to savor it.

Fingers curling into my hair, Darren breathed in my ear, "Put me where you want me, Piper."

A hand curled under my thigh, Darren angled my hips up while I guided him inside of me. A low satisfying groan came out of both of us, Darren's length filling me to the hilt. We sat there for a moment, both of us just enjoying the feeling. Then he began to move.

One foot up on the sink, I wrapped my other leg around his hips, trying to shove him deeper, harder, faster. It felt like all my pent up libido was coming out in a full-on rage right this very moment and I needed Darren to fulfill it.

"You know," Darren breathed between thrusts. "I'm not an expert."

"About what?" I gasped and ground my hips against his.

"But is this good for the baby?" He slowed down slightly, his words seeming to make him lose his momentum.

"No, no, it's fine," I reassured him. "Don't you dare stop."

Darren paused for a moment and then without warning lifted me up off the counter and carried me into the bedroom. I tried to move while we walked but it was almost impossible to get the right momentum.

Lowering me onto the bed, Darren didn't stop there. He flipped me over and pulled me up on my knees. "Now, it's your turn to kneel for me," he growled into my ear from behind. Then he was inside of me again and whatever response I had was dead on my tongue.

Each swipe of his cock inside of me felt like a million bolts of lightning zapping all over my body and focusing in on my most sensitive areas. My nipples ached and my breasts grew heavy. The insides of my thighs were coated with my own liquids making each thrust of Darren's hips an audible experience.

When I came this time, I saw actual stars behind my eyes, my whole body shuddering and spasming from the overwhelming feeling. Darren grunted and let out a curse before laying a trail of kisses down my spine.

"I have missed you," he murmured, sliding out of me and laying down on the bed beside me.

I sank down onto my side, facing him and croaked out, "Ditto."

CHAPTER 16

Allister

I DON'T KNOW HOW I got talked into this.

Why did I have to teach the fake Piper how to fight? She wasn't ever going to use it. I mean, the whole point of her being here was to keep the others from knowing the real Piper was gone, wasn't it? If she actually had to fight then we'd all be fucked, cause this witch might be good at spells but she couldn't throw a punch worth a shit.

"Alright now, punch with your left. Good. Now, your right." I held my hands up before me, demonstrating how Angelica should position her hands. "Now, make sure you shift your body with the movement. Don't just throw your fist out there, you have to turn your hips with it as well."

Angelica frowned and tried to do as I instructed her. Unfortunately, every punch she threw was like a dead fish. With her wrist bending, the likelihood that it was going to hurt anyone other than herself was growing lower and lower.

I sighed and waved her off. "Take a break."

"Great." Piper/Angelica breathed, dropping her arms and marching over to the bench where she chugged her bottle of water.

I stretched my arms over my head and then from one side to the other, trying to remind myself that this was important. Not only because of my Piper but in the line of work Angelica did she might not be able to use her magic and would need to be able to defend herself.

"Can I ask you something?"

Pausing in my stretches, I glanced over at Angelica. "Sure. What's up?"

"Do you all love this Piper chick?" She gestured at her glamoured body.

I frowned, my brows furrowed. "Of course. Why do you ask?"

Angelica shrugged and stretched her legs out in front of her. "Just seems a bit weird for one girl to be dating so many guys at once."

"You pretend to be other people's fantasies for money, how is that any less weird?" I shot back, not liking the judgment she was putting on us.

"Hey, I never said it wasn't creepy, but the pay is good and a girl's gotta eat." The more she talked the more her southern accent came out, making Piper's voice come out all weird.

"And you don't find that more strange than multiple men wanting to be with the same woman?" I picked up my silver container of blood and took a gulp of it.

"No..." Angelica trailed off, coming to her feet. "Lots of men want me but only a few at the same time. And none of them are practically brothers or in a pseudo homosexual relationship."

I almost choked on my blood. "What?" I coughed.

"Oh, you know..." she wiggled her finger toward the other part of the house. "The stuff going on with Antoine and Darren."

I shook my head. "You misunderstand. They're not gay."

Angelica shrugged. "Never said they were. I said pseudo homosexual relationship. They do have sex with women, correct?"

"Look, I'm not comfortable talking about this with you." I put the lid back on my canister and sat it back down. "Come on, let's work on your form more. You're gonna break your hand if you don't fix your wrist."

"Ugh," Angelica dragged herself toward me. In some ways she was exactly like Piper. She never liked practicing either. "When am I going to use this? I'm just supposed to wander around and pretend to clean."

"You only pretend to clean?"

"What?" Angelica's eyes widened and then she chuckled, "Pfft. What? No. I'm joking. Of course, I clean." Her eyes slid to the side.

I wasn't sure I believed her.

Shaking my head, I lifted my hands back up. "Come on, what else do you have to do?"

Throwing her hands up in the air, Angelica shook her head as well. "I guess you're right." She swung her arms from side to side and cracked her neck. "Jeez, I haven't had to put in this much physical effort since that group of baseball players came in last winter solstice."

I opened my mouth to ask about that comment when my brother came charging through the door.

"We've got a problem," Drake announced, glancing from Angelica to me. "Oh good, you're practicing. You're gonna need that."

"Huh, say what now?" Angelica dropped her hands and moved over to my brother. "I'm going to need what?"

Drake ignored her and looked at me. "Vincent wants Piper to start hunting again."

"He wants what now?" I gaped at him and then darted a look at Angelica before lowering my voice so she couldn't hear me. "She can't do that. They'll kill her."

"Her, is standing right here," Angelica shoved in between us with a glare. "And her agrees. This was supposed to be a low danger job." She crossed her arms over her chest. "I'm not going out to hunt vampires."

"You're not," I told her with a reassuring smile, then to my brother. "She's not, right? I mean what happened to finding the council? She can't do that and fight vampires."

Drake wrapped his arms around himself, gripping his elbows in either hand. "Apparently, she can. Cause they are under the impression that Piper's not actually figuring out where the council is located."

I narrowed my gaze on him. "And where would they get that idea from?"

Drake rolled his neck and dragged a hand over his head. "From me."

"What?" I gaped, smacking him over the side of the head. "Why would you even tell them that? The whole point is to keep Piper away from them, not closer to them."

Drake shot me a glare before turning his attention back to Angelica. "Look, that doesn't matter. What matters is that they're on their way over here now to pick Piper up."

"What?" Angelica's voice rose to a sharp pitch. "Pick me up to do what?"

Grimacing, Drake shrugged. "To fight vampires of course."

Angelica's mouth turned into an o-shape while she backed up and shook her head. "Ooooh, no no no. I did not sign up for this. I can't fight vampires. I can't even kill the spider in my bedroom at home. I just let my cat deal with them."

"But you have to," Drake implored, grabbing her hands with both his hands. "If you don't then they'll find out that Piper isn't really here and then she'll be in danger from both sides." He held her hands tightly, locking eyes with her. "Please. Do it for us. Do it for our unborn child."

I knew that look on Drake's face. He was trying to use his persuasion powers on her which in most cases I would have been against. Forcing someone to do something against their will, especially something this dangerous, would be a big no-no in my book…but it's Piper. And there were so many lines I would cross to keep her and our baby safe."

Unfortunately, Angelica didn't think the same.

"Don't you try to vampire magic woo me." Her hand swung out and smacked Drake across the face. She cried out and grabbed her hand. "Fuck. Fuck. Fuck. Fuck. What is your face made out of, bricks?"

Drake sighed and glanced over at me. "Hey, it was worth a shot."

A throat cleared at the training room door. We all turned to see Wynn standing in the doorway. "I'm not sure if you were aware but there are several frightening looking hunters standing in our foyer waiting for Piper to join them."

"Shit. They're already here?" Drake dragged his hands down his face in what would normally have been a comical way if the situation wasn't more crucial.

"Well, you can just tell them to fuck off," Angelica jumped in with a scowl. "I'm not going anywhere with them."

I sighed and turned to her. "Look, I know it's scary but it's easy, I promise. Just cut the head, stab the heart, easy peasy. And if nothing else, hide in the back and pretend."

Angelica gave me a skeptical look. "If it's so easy, why aren't more of you dead?"

I clicked my fingers and smacked my fist into my hand before a thought came to me. "Okay, how about this. We will pay you double?" Angelica arched a brow at me. "Okay, triple. We will triple your pay."

"Hey, now." Drake smacked me on the arm. "Offer her hazard pay."

I bobbed my gaze from Drake to Angelica. "Yeah, triple pay plus hazard pay."

Angelica pressed her lips tightly together and frowned. Her forehead scrunching together as she thought about our offer. After a long drawn out moment that felt like a lifetime, Angelica clicked her tongue and fake shot at me with her thumb and finger. "You got a deal. Let's go kill some vamps."

I sagged in relief as Angelica skipped out of the training room.

Drake shot a look at the empty doorway and then back to me with a worried frown. "How long do you give it before they figure out she's not really Piper?"

I glanced where he stared and reluctantly responded, "If we're lucky…more than five minutes."

CHAPTER 17

Piper

I SAT THERE STARING at the box that Darren had left me. It'd been two days and I couldn't bring myself to open it. Though, he had told me what was in it.

The blood of each one of my vampires.

But what was I supposed to do with it? I couldn't just pick an order and drink them one by one and hope that they were sleeping at that time.

I guess I could probably mix them up and just grab one at random, drink it, go to sleep, hope for the best? Then it would be kind of like a game. Who would I be banging tonight?

I sighed and leaned back on the couch.

Or maybe I should go to bed like normal and wait for Antoine to help me out. Maybe we could make up a schedule of some sorts.

However, twenty-four hours was not long enough of a time to see Darren.

I thought about going to Tuma to see about getting a longer extension or to see if one of the other guys could come and visit me but based on the way that Agnes was acting, I wasn't quite sure now was a good time.

I shot a curious look at her. Watching television as normal.

It was so frustrating. No one would tell me what was going on.

Every day, I would go about my normal routine: wake up, have breakfast with Agnes, maybe watch a little bit of TV, chat a little bit about her life or about my life. She asked me a little bit about Darren and how things were going and if I enjoyed my time with him. I had a feeling she wanted me to go into more detail. A little bit too personal for my taste but honestly, I had to talk to someone and Agnes seemed more on my side than on any of the vampire council sides.

So, I was starting to slowly yet hesitantly trust her. I'm not sure the trust was two ways.

Sometimes she'd look at me like what the hell was she doing here. Other times she seemed perfectly happy to be spending time with me rather than out scurrying about with the rest of the minions.

"So, what's going on?" I asked Agnes one day.

"What do you mean?" she asked, looking at me briefly before turning back to her medical comedy show.

I grabbed the remote from her and turned the TV off. Sitting on the coffee table in front of her, I grabbed her hands. "You know exactly what I'm talking about. Why is everybody tiptoeing around me. Why won't anyone tell me what's going on?"

Agnes hesitated.

"Come on," I urged her, squeezing her hands tightly. "I thought we were friends, why can't you tell me? I just want what's best for my baby and if I'm in trouble, or our lives are in danger I should know, don't you think?"

Agnes sighed and reluctantly turned to face me. "All right fine, there's something going on but you didn't hear it from me. Your vampires are making a big old fuss about wanting to see you and demanding things from the council that they don't want to do right now."

"What kind of things?"

"Oh," she breathed out, "you know. They want you to be let go. They want to be able to protect you themselves and they don't think the council is capable of doing it anymore." Agnes shook her head. "I don't know, my orders haven't changed. I'm supposed to stay with you, take care of you, make sure you're happy, give you companionship, and be here in case something happens with the baby." She arched her brow. "Nothing's happened with the baby, right?"

I placed my hand on my growing belly. "No, things are fine. Wow!" I started, staring down at my belly for a second.

What was that?" Agnes asked with a concerned look on her face.

"I think the baby just kicked. Here, feel it." I grabbed Agnes's hand and placed it over where mine was pressing onto my stomach.

After a few moments, I thought nothing was going to happen and then there it was. Like a tiny little burp.

"Why yes," Agnes smiled brightly. "You've got quite the energetic baby going on in there. Have you thought about names?"

I frowned. "No, I haven't. I don't know if it's a boy or a girl yet, so how am I supposed to know what name to call it?"

"Well, we can always find out."

"Like an ultrasound?"

"I'm not sure if I could get an ultrasound machine in here," she pursed her lips together in thought and then added, "but I know a few old fashioned ways of telling."

I looked at her with a skeptical look. "How accurate are those?"

Agnes shrugged. "About as accurate as they could be I suppose. All the ones I did when I was alive ended up being right, save one that was twins but either way it's something fun to do."

I thought about it for a moment. Did I really want to try to see if my baby was a boy or a girl based on some kind of old folklore? No, not really but honestly what other choice did I have and sitting here worrying about the guys was just going to make me anxious and that definitely wasn't good for the baby.

"Ok, fine." I finally gave in with a sigh. "Let's do it. What do we gotta do?"

"Well, you sit here and I'll go get the stuff. I'll just be a few minutes. I'll be right back." Agnes released my hands and jumped off the couch and went to the door. On the way out she bumped into someone and the words,

"Excuse me master," was my only clue as to who was waiting outside the door.

Caleb walked in shortly after, his face the bored expression that's been there since day one.

I wondered briefly how he became a vampire. Who in their right mind would pick somebody that looked like a run of the mill tax account to live forever?

"What's up Caleb?" I asked, trying to act like nothing was bothering me and that I wasn't dying to know what the guys had said to them.

Caleb stood before me with his hands behind his back, his face a blank canvas. His voice ever the monotone came out slowly and precisely, pronouncing each word as if it was a life-or-death situation. "I am sure that Agnes has told you now that your Durand vampires have been pestering myself and Master Tuma about being allowed to visit you."

"Okay," I drew out, "and is that any different from a normal day? I mean you've got the mother of their child locked up where they can't see her. Why would they not be upset?"

"I quite understand the human mind is full of emotional responses," Caleb explained as if I weren't a human. "Though I would expect vampires to have risen above those responses. Sadly, it seems that your vampires have not quite evolved into my current state of being."

"Not even dinosaur bones have evolved to your current state," I muttered to myself.

Nevertheless, I tried to change the conversation. "What did you want? I've got things to do." I stood up and moved around the room as if I really did have something to do other than wait anxiously for Agnes to come back with her little test.

Caleb stayed by the door as if it would pain him to step any further into my living quarters. "I simply wish to inform you of our response to your vampires' inquiries. We have reassured them repeatedly that we have you well in hand and you will be well protected on our grounds. I hope that you will pass this along to your master, Antoine, during your next dream encounter."

I froze. "What dream encounters?"

Caleb's lips twitched, not quite a smile but enough of a reaction to tell me that he could read the bullshit I was spewing.

"Please do not insult me by thinking that we do not know that you have been in contact with your master. We all know the side effects of becoming a human servant."

Well shit.

"Ok," I said, trying not to show that he had me rattled. "Anything else?"

Caleb turned to leave and then stopped. "Oh yes, one more thing. If those hunter friends of yours try to attack us or if we find out that your vampires have disclosed our location to them in any way, we will kill you. Have a good night."

He left, shutting the door with a firm hand.

Well, that freaking sucks.

How was I going to tell them that the plan was off?

How was I going to tell them that we were pretty much screwed?

If we didn't tell the vampire hunters where I was located or where the council was located then they were going to kill my guys and if we did tell them the council would kill me and my baby. I really was stuck between a hunter and a vampire.

Angus walked back in a moment later, happy as a clam. Completely clueless that I had just had my life and the life of my child threatened.

Smiling broadly, she held up a string and an old coin on it. "Who's ready to find out what they're having?"

I forced a smile on my face and reluctantly came over to her and sat on the couch. If anything, at least let's take my mind off of what was going on now. I just had to figure out a different way for us to get me out of here. "I'm ready." I replied, while my insides screamed, not even close.

CHAPTER 18

Drake

"SO HOW DO YOU think Angelica's doing being a hunter?" Rayne asked, lounging back on the couch.

"You mean, how is she surviving?" I pointed out with a chuckle, offering up a fist bump to my twin.

Allister gave my fist bump a sardonic look before turning to the television.

"Oh, come on, you know you're the one that convinced her to do it. You could at least be a little happy we got away with it for a little bit longer. I mean Angelica has to suck it up and she gets to be a hunter but she also gets triple pay and hazard pay. This keeps Piper and the baby safe and in my opinion that's a win-win."

"I do not think Angelica feels the same way," Wynn pointed out from his bed, not looking away from his book.

I looked over the couch at Wynn, giving him a flat stare. "Hey, none of you had any other ideas. I figured it out, got us out of a shitty situation. We just have to buy our time until we can get Piper out of the council's hideout."

Allister snorted, "And whose fault is it that we were in that position in the 1st place? Oh right, that was you."

Marcus, who had not said anything, spoke up as he went to the mini fridge by his bed. "I think it is a horrible idea, endangering an innocent girl's life just for our own ends."

I scoffed, "And what would you have us do? Rush in with our balls in our hands just waiting for the council to slice them off? I don't think so. I like my balls firmly where they are." Adjusting them in my pants.

"In Piper's purse, you mean," Rayne chuckled.

"And like yours aren't? If any of us are whipped it's you," I pointed out to Rayne with a punch to his shoulder.

"Hey knock it off," Rayne shoved me away. "It's not my fault that she likes me best." He paused and grinned. "Actually, it's a bit my fault." He slid his hands down his body. "Can't help what I was born with."

"Who says she likes you best?" I argued. "Why would she like a scrawling little thing like you when she can have all this plus two." I gestured between myself and Allister.

"Leave me out of this," Allister said from his side of the couch, adding on, "I'm not worried about who she likes best."

"That's because you already had your little hissy fit. It's our turn," I pointed out to him.

"Well, she does have the vials of our blood," Wynn pointed out from his bed. "Perhaps we shall see who exactly Piper likes best by seeing who she chooses first."

Rayne scoffed, "Why? You already know who she chose first. She chose Darren. Wasn't it him she chose to visit her in person while the rest of us get second hand dream visits?"

"Now, now," Wynn tried to reassure Rayne, "We all know the reason she chose Darren was because he's the only one that seemed less threatening to the vampire council and might I add, the only one that would not be able to see her in a dream. The rest of us could see her anytime we like as long as she has our blood in her system."

"Yeah, but whose blood is she going to drink first?" I inquired with a cock of my head. "How are we going to know if tonight is the night, or the day I suppose, that she drinks our blood."

"I say, we bet on it."

"Wait, what?" I looked over at Marcus in surprise. "Are you seriously suggesting that we bet on who Piper picks first to see the dream?"

Marcus shrugged his shoulders but didn't retract his statement.

"What do you know that we don't know?" I asked, never taking my eyes off the larger vampire.

Marcus's expression didn't waver. "I am simply not as unsure of Piper's love for me as the rest of you are."

"Speak for yourself, *mon ami.*" Wynn jumped in with a smirk. "I am well aware of Piper's love for me. She has bestowed it upon me many times."

"Sucking your dick is not the same thing as being in love with you," I shot back with a smug look. "If that were the case then I would definitely be the highest on her list."

Alister shook his head, closing his eyes with a disgusted look on his face. "I can't believe we're even talking about this. If Piper were here —"

"But she's not," I interrupted him. "So, what do you think? Should we bet on it?"

"Fine," Alister sighed, throwing his head back against the back of the couch. "If everybody's doing it then I guess I can too."

"Ok," Rayne clapped his hands and rubbed them together. "What are we gonna bet? Money? Blood? Pieces of property?"

"I think we should make it more interesting," Wynn said, closing his book with his finger in his place to scan the rest of us.

"Like what?" I asked.

He lifted one finger up to his lips in a hush movement. "Secrets."

"Secrets? We know each other's secrets already," I returned with a laugh. "Make it a little bit more challenging."

"I do not know about the rest but I do know that I have not disclosed every secret of my human and vampire life," Wynn explained, scanning over the others looking for their reaction.

None of the others protested.

I frowned.

"Come on, you can't be serious. I thought we were brothers. How can you have secrets from your brothers? You know, Allister and I don't have any secrets from each other."

Alister cleared his throat.

"Alister," I said, staring at my twin. "You can't seriously say there's something you haven't told me."

Allister scratched the back of his neck; he looked off to the side, guilt clearly written all over his face.

I scowled, "Fine. It seems as if I'm the only one not keeping anything back, what am I going to bet?"

"Oh, I'm sure even you have something." Rayne snickered from the side, seeming quite sure of himself.

"Why do you even care? You could just look up all our stuff online," I gestured to the red head with a glare

"Not things that were before the Internet," Rayne pointed out and then paused to think about it for a second. "Actually, I probably could find quite a few things on the Internet from before. I've found images of us online before, though they don't know who we are."

"Okay, okay. Fine, secret keepers, who do we think?" I glanced around the room to get some kind of idea of who thought they were gonna go first.

"I for one think it's going to be Wynn," Allister said with a sort of sad shrug.

"Wynn? Why do you think it will be him?" I scowled. "Why not me? Or me and Allister. I mean she could get two for one with us."

"You said that already. And believe me two for one is not always the best," Rayne shook his head with a smirk. "Sometimes a woman just wants to be loved and made love too. Not pounded into the ground between two meatheads."

"Who are you calling a meathead, you big old nerd."

"Hey, now let's not argue between ourselves. Who do you think?" Allister asked.

I crossed my arms over my chest, my lips tugging up on one side. "I think it'll be me and you. Has to be. Makes no sense otherwise."

"Okay, Wynn, what do you think?" Allister asked, turning away from me.

Allister hummed and stared off into the distance.

Wynn nonchalantly said, "I think it will be Rayne."

"Really?' Rayne asked, his voice going high pitched. "Why do you think it will be me?"

Wynn rolled his head slowly to the side, staring at us on the couch. "It is simple mathematics. Out of the six of us you are far closer to Piper's emotional maturity and at the current moment... What is she six-seven months along? She is probably feeling quite old right now. And as the youngest of us, Rayne would be the obvious choice to make her feel as if she were a younger woman again."

I snorted. "If that's your explanation then she should have just kept Darren. He's closer to her age and he's a human."

"No, no, he's not," Rayne argued. "Dear Darren might be a human but he's older than me by like a hundred and fifty years."

"Oh right," I paused, thinking about that for a moment. "I forgot because you look like such a dumb-ass punk."

"You really need to stop watching cable television," Allister muttered. "You're losing all of your aristocratic upbringing."

I shrugged. "It wasn't that great when I was alive, why do I need it now?"

"What about you Marcus? What do you think?" Rayne asked, interrupting our conversation.

Marcus sat on the edge of his bed drinking from the blood canister. "Well my heart tells me that it will be me but my head tells me it is more likely to be Wynn.”

“Jesus fuck,” I cried out, throwing myself back on the couch. “What the fuck is so great about Wynn? Why does he get all the women?”

The man himself was about to answer when there was a loud thud from the front door slamming shut and then Piper's voice screaming for us to get up there.

I blinked up at the ceiling. “Sounds like Angelica's home and not happy.”

CHAPTER 19

Wynn

"EVERYBODY GET IN HERE right now!" Angelica screamed from the front door.

Everyone hurried out of the basement towards the screaming. I slowly set my book on the side table, placing a bookmark in it and casually standing from my bed.

The only woman that I rushed for was Piper and she was nowhere to be found. This look alike left much to be desired. She might look like Piper and at times she might act like Piper but she was no Piper.

No, my Piper was off somewhere else. Off somewhere else alone and pregnant. During my human time, a male might be concerned for her fragile state but not me. I've seen what Piper can do. I know how well she can hold her own. And while I mourn the loss of her embrace, the feel of her kiss, the taste of her blood on my tongue, I knew that rushing in would only make things worse for her.

My only wish was that this was over already. So that I may have her in my arms again and our babe to dote on. We could watch it grow together however long its lifespan may be.

I did not want to sit around and cater to the whims of some human witch that did not seem to get Piper or our arrangement.

"Hurry up, Wynn," Rayne yelled down the stairs at me.

Letting out a sigh, I made my way up the stairs. I wondered what the little witch was crying out about now. It couldn't be much. She didn't have much of a job. Though, I admit, the hunting of vampires was not something that she had signed up for. I could give her credit for her distress in that.

I walked through the dining room and into the foyer to see Piper, no Angelica, standing there in Piper's clothes. A pair of leather pants and tank top attire that I had quite enjoyed a few times with my wily little human maid but on the little witch made me irritated. Not to forget the sting of blood that filled my nose from blood that covered the cloth and face of the fake Piper.

"What happened to you?" Drake asked, coming closer to the witch.

"Where's Darren?" she cried out in her southern twang, her arms crossed over her chest and then she dropped them when she realized she was just getting more blood on herself.

"I don't know, probably boinking Antoine in his office or something," Drake replied, looking over her and then sniffing the air. "Is that vampire blood?"

"Yes," fake Piper snarled at Drake, "You'll be happy to know I killed my first vampire today and I'll tell you how I felt — I hated it. It was disgusting. Blood got everywhere and it is totally killing my karma. I'm a witch. I'm not supposed to be killing people. You know what comes around goes around and all that jazz." She continued to rant on with a stomp of her foot. "I did not sign up for this. Screw the triple pay. Screw the hazard pay. I'm going home and washing myself for fifty million years and I don't know...search for some spell that will sanitize my soul enough to get this stank off of me."

"Now, just hold on a moment," Allister said, trying to calm the witch down. "This is part of the job. You knew you were going to have to kill a vampire, right? You agreed to that when you went out hunting with them."

"No," she wagged her finger in Allister's face. "I agreed to pretend to go hunting with them. I did not say that I was actually going to hunt anybody. I don't hunt anything. Not animals. Not people. And certainly not vampires." She threw her hands up with a high pitched screech. "I am a fucking stripper, a prostitute at worst. I get paid to suck people off, to pretend to be their fantasies. I do not get paid to chop vampire's heads off!"

"I understand where you're coming from, *mon cher*." I came up to the witch, trying to help take the edge off of the traumatizing experience she just encountered.

I suppose it was a good thing to find out that she did not enjoy killing vampires because then we would have another hunter on our hands. Then again it also put us in a precarious situation because I believe that the witch was about two seconds away from quitting. She'd march right through that door, putting us right back to where we were in the first place.

"No, you don't get it. I quit! I'm not doing this. This isn't my job. Tell Darren to lose my number." She shoved past us and then paused. "Actually, don't tell anyone anything. I'm changing my number. I'm changing my name. I am going to disappear. I don't want anything to do with you vampires ever again. That's it, I'm done."

"And here I thought Piper was dramatic," Drake muttered under his breath.

"But what about Piper and the baby," Allister brought up, no doubt trying to appeal to her feminine side. "Are you just going to let them get hurt because of this?"

"No offense," she half turned a hand on the stair banister, "but that's not my problem. She's your lady, it's your baby, you figure it out. I am not Piper, it is not my baby. I wanna go home and that's exactly where I'm going right after I clean this shit off of me."

Angelica stomped up the stairs, leaving us standing there dumbfounded.

"Well, what the fuck are we going to do now?" Drake asked the group, always the eloquent one.

"Yes," a feminine voice came from the open front door. "Please do tell. What do you plan to do now that your plan has failed?"

All of our heads turned to the front door, a feeling of horror overcoming me. There stood Mizuki and all of her battle splendor, a burning rage in her dark eyes. Those same eyes went up to the stairs, where a fake Piper had disappeared and then back to us.

"I knew something fishy was going on with you guys. That Piper is nothing like the Piper I know. Where did you even pick this chick up from?" Mizuki pulled a dagger from her belt and flipped it over in her hand. An action that was meant to be intimidating, and it worked.

Drake chuckled, shaking his head. "You wouldn't believe us if we told you."

Mizuki pointed the dagger towards his neck, narrowing her gaze on him. "Try me."

Drake stared down at the dagger, a nervous chuckle coming from him. "A strip club."

"And where is the real Piper?"

Drake glanced around at the others looking for some kind of sign of what he should say. I was at my wits end. I had no idea what we could say in this instance. She'd caught us quite literally red handed. Or rather caught Angelica red handed.

"We should just come clean, *mon amis.* We are going to need their assistance now more than ever and I suggest that we make good on our promise to instruct them on where to find the vampire council. Do you not?" I glanced at the others with a pointed look.

Rayne and Marcus seemed more than happy to let the hunters in on where Piper was though it had always been Marcus's opinion that we go storming and get her ourselves. Now it seems that he would get what he wanted and then some.

"How do you know that we even know where she's at?" Allister asked silkily, his powers tickling my nose. "For all you know we could be as much in the dark as you are."

Mizuki ignored it. "Don't think that I'm some simpleton who doesn't know what you're capable of. It all started with that vampire council and I bet that they are the ones that have Piper. So where are they?"

Look," Marcus said, taking charge. "We know where Piper is, we even know how many guards are watching her, we know the layout of the place, we even know the rotation of the guards, we can tell you all of this."

"You can bet your asses. You better tell me where or you'll be the ones that end up on the bad end of a stake," Mizuki threatened, turning that dagger towards him.

Marcus grabbed the dagger by the blade, letting it bite into his skin, the blood dripping down his arm and onto the floor. Mizuki locked eyes with him not bothered by his actions

"We'll tell you on one condition."

"I'm listening."

"We get to come with you."

CHAPTER 20

Piper

I WALKED AROUND THE courtyard, circling around the fountain with my usual guard as my shadow, my mind full of doubt and worry.

Antoine wasn't in my dreams again.

It was one of the first times that I assumed he would be there and then he wasn't. Though, I could chalk it up to him being busy but something inside of me was telling me something was wrong.

There had to be a reason why he wasn't there today. It had been a few weeks since

Caleb's threatening words. I'd been anxious to tell Antoine what he'd said. On the other hand, I didn't want them to do anything rash and get us all killed.

And yet Antoine still has not been in my dreams. What is he doing? Why isn't he showing up?

Stroking a hand over my stomach, I looked forlornly down at my growing bump. I couldn't see my feet anymore. Something I hadn't expected to miss until I couldn't.

It seems like my baby's growth has gone into hyper drive over the last few weeks. Agnes didn't know how to explain it. Though to be fair, she has never had a human servant pregnant before.

"What do you think your daddies are doing?" I asked the baby in my stomach. It turned around and pressed on my bladder. "Yes, I guess as much."

Agnes's little trick with the coin and the string didn't exactly work. It didn't really go any decisive way that would tell me if it was a boy or a girl. Agnes had told me that tended to happen sometimes. Especially with unusual pregnancies. She also said that it could mean that I am having twins or triplets. The very thought of it made me want to vomit.

I hope the fuck not.

I never thought I would hope that I had a vampire baby that would eat its way out of my stomach rather than having multiple ones. I could hardly handle the thought of one let alone the thought of twins. Or God forbid, triplets.

"Should you be pacing like that?" My guard asked, one of the few words he's ever said to me.

I waved him off. "It's fine. I've done waaay more exerting activities just a few weeks ago.

"I do not want you passing out on my watch. You know, they will blame me." The way his face paled and his eyes darted around us made me feel bad.

"Fine," I sighed, sitting on the side of the fountain. Everybody was worried about me but nobody was worried about my vampires. Nobody but me that was.

Once I sat down on the edge of the fountain, I realized my mistake. It was going to be impossible for me to get back up without the help of the guard. I guess I could just sit here for a while. Better than making both of us look foolish.

I thought today that I would try and take the blood of some of the guys and see if maybe I could get ahold of one of them in their dreams. Problem was that I didn't want to waste it and not get anything out of it.

Maybe I could ask Tuma for a day pass or cell phone. Something. I was going crazy just sitting here waiting to hear something from someone.

Then again, I probably shouldn't know anything since Caleb was able to read my mind. Fuck. I hadn't thought about that. If I knew what was going on then he'd know what the plan was and put us all in danger.

No.

I sagged in my seat by the fountain, getting even more upset as I thought about it. It was probably better for me not to know anything about the plan. But it was just so...ugh... frustrating.

I hated sitting here twiddling my thumbs like a hopeless maiden. I hadn't been helpless since before we went into hiding.

The whole point of me learning to fight and becoming a hunter was so that I would never have to feel this way again.

I tried to lean forward onto my elbows with my hands on my face but my belly got in the way. Letting out a growl of frustration, I jumped up to my feet, something that surprised even me.

"What is it?" My guard asked his eye searching around the area for some sign of danger.

I scowled at him, "Nothing. I'm fine."

"Don't scare me like that. If something happens to you then I'm the one that's going to get in trouble. And I like my head where it is," he shot me a glaring look.

"I know, I'm sorry." I turned my back on the guard and wandered around the courtyard for a little longer. The sun was starting to set and soon my companion would be back at my side and I wouldn't have time to sit alone.

A crow cawed.

Frowning, I walked towards the sound and glanced up into a nearby tree where a single crow sat on the branch.

Strange. Normally there weren't any animals in the courtyard. I'd always assumed it was their natural instinct to stay away because of the predators lurking in the building around them. But this crow didn't seem to be bothered by that, in fact it seemed to be staring straight at me.

My eyes widened and it came to me.

I walked closer to the tree and glanced around back at my guard before back to the crow. "Antoine," I whispered, hoping I was right. Otherwise, I was going to look like a complete idiot talking to a bird. "Is that you?"

Antoine let out a little caw, fluttering his wing slightly.

Something fell to the ground.

Making sure no one was watching me, I bent over and picked it up, tucking it into the pocket of my dress. None of my clothing fit anymore and I had to borrow some clothes that Agnes had found lying around.

I begged her to let me shop online or something but Tuma was too worried that I was going to send out some kind of distress signal to the others.

Fucking coward.

I turned back to the crow, hoping to get some kind of answer from him but before I could ask anything else he opened his wings and flew away.

I walked two steps toward it, wanting to call out to stop him but I didn't want to draw attention to him or myself.

Well crap. What was it going to do now?

If Antoine was showing up in his crow form, then that could only mean something was wrong. Something that made it so that he couldn't come see me in my dreams.

I palmed the note in my pocket as I walked back to the guard. I wanted so badly to look at it right now but I couldn't risk it.

"I'm ready to go back now," I told my guard.

"Already? We haven't been out here for more than ten minutes. I usually have to drag you back in." My guard arched his brow at me.

"I'm tired," I pretended to yawn. "I think I want to go lay down."

The guard surveyed the courtyard once more before jerking his head towards the entrance, "Alright let's go."

I tried my best to keep my footsteps normal and to not run ahead, dashing into my bedroom, so I could read the note in my pocket.

If the guard realized anything was amiss, he didn't say anything.

Once I got to my bedroom door at last, my hand instantly went to the doorknob. I moved to go inside, but the guard stopped me.

"Hold on now."

"What?" I asked, my words coming out more aggravated and impatient than I meant.

"Are you going to want to go for another walk when you get up from your nap?"

I paused and thought about it for a moment. "I'll have to let you know. I don't know. If you're busy I'll just get Agnes to take me."

"Very well," he nodded and turned on his heel, walking away from me. He was no doubt happy to go about his own business and not have to babysit the pregnant human servant.

I waited there a moment watching as he walked away and then turned the doorknob and walked into the room. Slowly, I closed the door and locked it.

With my eyes forward I moved what I hoped was naturally into my room, acting as if there wasn't something burning in a hole in my pocket at the very moment. I didn't trust that the cameras wouldn't see me looking at the note.

Slipping into the bathroom, I closed the door behind me, locking it for good measure. I didn't know if there were cameras in here but I had nowhere else to do this and I couldn't wait any longer.

Digging my hand into my pocket, I pulled out the little slip of paper Antoine had dropped.

It was not very big, about two by four inches. Its edges were all scraggly as if it had been ripped off a piece of paper in a hurry. On that piece of paper was Antoine's curly handwriting.

They're coming. Be ready.

I stared down at the words for a few more moments before crumbling up the piece of paper and throwing it in the toilet, flushing it.

Who is coming? The Durands? The hunters? Someone else? And how was I supposed to get ready? I had nothing here to fight against whoever was coming. Tuma and the others had made sure that I wasn't armed in any way. Even my silverware was plastic.

The situation must be dire if Antoine risked coming here just to give me the note. I chewed on my lower lip as I thought, my hand caressing my stomach. Either way I had to be ready.

CHAPTER 21

Antoine

"WELL…HOW'D SHE TAKE it?" Drake asked as we all huddled together in a corner of the room where the hunters were planning the attack on the vampire council.

The hunters had decided that tonight would be the night. Normally, they would have waited and gone during the daytime but since Marcus had smartly bartered with Mizuki for the vampire council's location for our participation in the raid, they had to move the attack to just before dawn. It wouldn't do well for us to burn up while trying to get Piper out of there.

"She received our note and seemed quite anxious to speak to us," I explained to him, brushing my sleeves off as I readjusted to my human form.

"Of course, she's anxious to speak to us. We've been giving her the cold shoulder for weeks now." Rayne snorted. "We didn't even get to have our little dream fuck fests like we had planned."

"Yes, I will be sure to pass on your sentiments to Piper while we are in the process of rescuing her," I said dryly.

"Stop your whining," Drake nudged Rayne in the arm. "None of the rest of us got any nookie time either."

"Antoine and Darren did," Rayne argued, nudging him back.

"And as soon as we rescue her, you'll have plenty of nookie time before the baby gets here," Drake grabbed Rayne by the shoulders, hugging him to the side with a chuckle.

"You better get what you can get before the baby gets here. Because from what I remember they take quite a bit of time and attention," Alister reminded all of us with a small frown.

"I'm not worried about it," Rayne waved him off. "There's enough of us here that the baby will have someone with it all the time and then Piper will have plenty of time to rest and we can all get reacquainted with her."

"I don't think that she's going to want to have any kind of reacquaintance time after having the baby. Don't they have to wait a certain amount of time before it's safe for them to have sex," Allister pointed out.

Wynn arched a brow. "There are other things that you can do that do not require penetration."

"You got that right," Drake laughed.

"Are we really talking about having sex with Piper before we've even got her back? What is wrong with you people?" Allister shook his head with a groan.

"Allister is right, let us focus on getting Piper back and then we can focus on the rest of it afterwards," I instructed them with a commanding look.

Tristan and Mizuki walked towards us just then and we went quiet.

Tristan turned to us with a grin. "Are you guys ready?"

Marcus shrugged and Drake cheered, "As ready as we ever are going to be."

Tristan grinned and smacked his fist into his open palm. "I bet you guys are ecstatic to take out the head honchos."

I skimmed the faces of my brothers, hoping that my expression would warn them to be careful with what they said.

"Honestly," Drake commented, "with what they have done to us with Piper I am more than ready to chop some heads off."

To my surprise, the others nodded their agreement.

I did nothing of the sort.

While I agreed that the council needed to be taken out, I did realize the implications that would put on us when a new council was elected to take their place, and there would be a new council. This wasn't the first council that had been overthrown and it wouldn't be the last.

"Why the long face, Antoine?" Mizuki asked, ever the watchful one. Nothing seemed to get past her.

Adjusting my cufflinks, I avoided her gaze. "Just anxious to get this over with and get Piper back home."

"Understandable. We would like Piper back as well. She is one of our best hunters." Mizuki nodded to Tristan who agreed with an eager bob of his head.

"You do realize she's not going to be able to hunt with you anymore since she's —" Rayne clapped a hand over Drake's mouth.

"Since the deal we have with your boss, Vincent, remember? We find the vampire council, deliver them to you, and you leave Piper and the rest of us alone." Rayne reminded her and everyone with a meaningful look.

Mizuki stared at Rayne and Drake with a suspicious glare. "We'll see about that."

The two of them walked away, leaving us to ourselves once more.

Rayne released Drake finally with a scowl. "What the fuck are you doing? You almost told them about Piper being pregnant. They don't need to know that."

"Fuck, Sorry," Drake scrubbed his face and placed his hands on his hips. "I got too caught up in the moment and forgot who I was talking to."

"Speaking of Vincent," Rayne brought back up, glancing around the area. "Where is he?"

I jerked my head to another part of the room. "Over there. Preening for his court.".

"How do we know he's going to keep his part of the deal?" Wynn asked, worry etched over his face.

"We don't," I told him, my gaze turning hard on the leader of the hunter's guild, "but accidents do happen."

"All right, everybody, I hope you're ready because we're going in now, we're going in hard and fast. Kill anyone you see with fangs," Mizuki told the group.

I cleared my throat loudly.

Albeit reluctantly, she added on, "Except for the Durands. Look at their faces, memorize them. Now let's go." We followed after them as we all piled into a series of vehicles. We decided to take our own for the sake of safety. The ride was silent and tense. None of us able to get out of our heads long enough to talk to each other.

"I have a bad feeling about this," Rayne muttered beside me as we hustled out of the armored vehicle behind the hunters. We decided to let them take the charge and to come in after so as not to let ourselves get mixed in with the enemy.

"Just stay close and follow Darren's instructions. We'll get to Piper and we'll get out of there. Let them take care of each other," I reassured him, focusing on the path ahead.

"Easy for you to say. He's not the one that has to go in with the hunters to save Piper." Drake growled from behind me.

"Someone had to stay behind in case something happened," I reminded him. "It could not be one of us."

"It just seems unfair," Drake grumbled.

"Less complaining, more searching," I called over my shoulder.

We stepped into the council's stronghold, the scent of blood strong in the air. The six of us tensed. My fangs ached at the copper smell of blood. I pushed the bloodlust aside and focused on looking for Piper.

"If Darren's instructions are correct," I began, keeping a look out for an attack. "We only have to go through those doors and down the hallway to the left and then a few other turns and then we will find her."

Unfortunately, a group of vampires were fighting a group of hunters right in front of the doorway.

"Yeah, easier said than done," Allister muttered as we started in that direction. "Just don't get staked in the process."

"Oh, live a little, brother," Drake chuckled as he swatted a human servant out of the way. "When do we get to actually go out and fight? Everything's so easy nowadays. You can order your blood online or you can even order a girl to your house. We haven't had to actually get down and dirty by fighting in a long time. Don't you miss the rush?"

Allister snorted, shoving another human servant out of the way and then he grabbed a vampire in a headlock. "You seem to forget, brother, I was not the one that enjoyed fighting, that was you. I prefer to be more civilized and use my words."

Drake snapped his neck and shoved the body away from him. "What's so civilized about arguing over stupid stuff that's just going to turn into a fight anyways?"

I pushed between the twins and grabbed for the double doors. "If you two are done debating over the right way to settle an argument. I believe Piper is waiting for us."

The others followed after me while the twins and Marcus finished up the rear. My tension was so focused on which way Darren had told me to go that I didn't notice the hunter that was sneaking up behind me.

"Antoine, watch out," Wynn jumped in between us, taking a stake into his upper left chest.

"Fuck. That stings," Wynn groaned and grasped at the stake, pulling it from his chest and then throwing it back at the hunter who had missed his heart. Wynn did not miss and hit the hunter straight in the chest.

"Thank you, my friend," I patted Wynn on the shoulder. "Come, let us find Piper and get you taken care of."

Wynn pressed his hand over his wound and stumbled after me, the others keeping an eye out so that we could make sure that Wynn didn't get hurt any further.

"Why is it always you that seems to be the one that ends up getting hurt in these situations," Rayne pointed out with a frown.

"What can I say?" Wynn explained with a voice full of pain. "I simply love too dearly."

"Yeah," Drake pointed out. "One of these days that love's gonna end up with you on the wrong end of a stake... oh wait...that already happened."

Wynn snorted and then coughed a laugh. "You would not be so quick to judge me when one of these days the stake I'll be taking is for you."

"You're right, I'm sorry," Drake shot back as he hit another hunter that had decided that he wanted to take us out in the midst of a fight.

"These hunters don't seem to care that we're on their side," Alister pointed out with a frown.

"I don't think they really care one way or the other. They just want to get rid of vampires. We're vampires. They're doing their job," I told him while searching for the next turn.

"Well, at least we are prepared for them and we're not being taken by surprise like the others," Marcus supplied before turning around. "Is this the right way?"

I sniffed the air, "Yes, Piper's this way."

Not much further now and we would have Piper in our grasp. I only hoped we got there first.

CHAPTER 22

Piper

I SAT ON THE couch in my bedroom, flickering through the channels on the television trying to find something to distract me from the anxiety of waiting for the hunters to finally attack when Angus came bursting through the bedroom door.

"Get up, you need to get going," she grabbed at me from the couch and I scrambled to my feet.

"What's going on? What's happening?" She tried to pull me towards the door and I dragged my feet behind me.

"The vampire hunter's found us. We have to get you out of here."

"Wait a second, they're not going to hurt me." I told her, pulling my arm away from her. "I was one of them, don't you remember? If you stay with me, I'll protect you."

Agnes paused, turning back to me and her back to the door. "It's not them I'm worried about. Remember what will happen to you if they find us?"

"Yeah, I remember what Caleb said, but I can't let you get yourself hurt by trying to help me. You have to get out of here. They won't stop to think about whether or not you're a good vampire; they'll just kill you."

The sound of fighting grew closer to the doorway the longer we spoke. Worry covered Agnes's face and I saw that she struggled with what she should do. Suddenly she stuck her hand in her pocket and pulled something out and handed it to me. "Here, take this, it will at least provide you with some kind of protection if Caleb comes for you."

I took what she handed to me, my eyes moving from her face down to my hands quickly before going back up to hers. "A stake. How did you get a stake?"

"Don't worry about that right now, worry about keeping you and your baby safe." Agnes glanced down at my stomach and then back to my face.

"What about you? Where are you going to go? You could stay here, I'll protect you."

"Not if you can't protect yourself from Caleb. He's my master. I have to do what he says. If he told me to turn on you, I would have to."

That did present a problem. I blew out of breath and rubbed my forehead with my fingers. "Then what are you going to do?"

"There is an escape route through the basement that'll lead me out of here. I'll get out of here through there. You just worry about getting yourself and the baby out."

I grabbed her hands, keeping her from leaving. An emotion overwhelmed me for a moment. "Will I ever see you again? I feel like this time we've been together has been..."

"I know I feel the same way too." Agnes squeezed my hands, a sad smile coming across your face.

I opened my mouth to say something else but then her expression changed to surprise and then pain overcame her face. I jumped back as the sharp point of a stake came out the front of her chest.

Agnes grunted and her hands went to the stake before she glanced back up at me once more and then fell to the ground dead.

Caleb stood behind her. A calm expression on his face. "I told you what would happen if they found us."

"Now hold on a moment," I backed up, holding the stake that Agnes had given me behind my back. "Have you spoken to Tuma and Odetta about this? Are they okay with you killing me because how am I supposed to know that they were going to come? I didn't tell them to come."

"You can't lie to me, Piper. I can read your mind. I know and you know that you told your little vampire lovers where to find you and of course they could not keep their mouths shut and now here we have the vampire hunters on our doorstep or rather in the foyer down the hall. Now either you can let me kill you or let them kill you."

I snorted and smiled. "What makes you think they're coming to kill me? I'm the one they're coming to save. It's you who should be worried."

Caleb's lips curled up into the first smile I'd ever seen on his face and it wasn't a pleasant one. "Either way, you'll be dead before they get here."

He dashed for me, his fangs bared at me.

I pulled the stake out from behind my back and dodged left, swiping at him but missing.

Damn he was fast.

I ran around the bed. Caleb came at me from one side. I jumped over the mattress and scrambled away from him but Caleb was right there nipping at my heels.

"The longer you draw this out the more it will hurt," Caleb explained in a bored tone that made it seem like killing me was just an everyday task like cleaning the dishes or taking out the trash.

I darted for the door. Caleb blocked my way. The only other way out was through the bathroom and even then, I didn't think that I could get through the tiny hole in the window.

Still, I had to try.

I ran into the bathroom, slamming the door behind me, locking it for good measure. Though, I knew it was pointless. I searched around the bathroom for something that I could use against him. The only thing that was in here was the box of blood that Darren had given me and that wasn't going to do anything, not to another vampire anyway.

In this instance, I wish I wasn't pregnant. Out of this entire time there had only been a few times that I had been upset about the prospect of having a child but now it was becoming an overwhelming health hazard.

If I wasn't pregnant then I could have taken out Caleb. If I wasn't pregnant then I wouldn't even be here in the first place.

What the fuck, what does it matter? I'm pregnant, there's nothing I could do about it now. I just had to suck it up and figure this out on my own.

Caleb banged at the door. "Come out of there, don't make me break it down. Tuma will be very cross with me if I break the door."

"Too damn bad," I shouted back. I wished Tuma had more of a concern for me than the status of an inanimate object.

He banged on the door a few more times and it cracked.

For a moment, I thought that it was all over. That this was the moment that I was going to die and my baby was going to die and I'd never get to see it be born. I'd never see its cute little face. I'd never get to see its little fingers curling around my own. I'd never get to know what the baby's gender was or to pick out a name.

My fingers curled around the stake in my hand tightly, my back straightening. No, I wasn't going to go down without a fight. This was it. It was either me or Caleb and I was determined it wasn't going to be me.

Caleb's foot shot through the door and half of the door ended up littered across the floor. I braced myself to rush at him, hoping to get him while he was stuck in the door fragments. Before I could reach him, he was jerked out of the wood of the door and pulled back into the bedroom. There was the telltale sound of a slice and then something hit the floor with a thud.

I waited in the bathroom, holding my breath as I waited for whoever the newest enemy was to descend on me. Then a familiar face poked through the hole in the door.

Vincent.

He smiled, looking me over, his eyes landing on my large belly. "Would you look at that? This is quite a surprise."

I gave a nervous laugh, waving slightly but not putting down the stake. "Oh, hey fancy meeting you here."

"Do you want to open the door," Vincent asked, nodding his head towards the doorknob a few inches away from him, "or should I?"

"No, no," I shook him off, heading for the door. "I'll come out. I'll come out." I didn't want to be backed into a corner any longer than I had been. At least, faced with my frenemy I had a chance of getting away.

Vincent moved away from the door and I unlocked it, pushing what remained of it out of the way. It kind of fell sideways against the wall with a cracking sound.

I stepped into the bedroom and my eyes immediately found Caleb's body lying on the floor, his head rolling around a few feet away. Mizuki was standing nearby cleaning her sword off with a rag. While Tristan stood close behind her.

Mizuki took one look at my pregnant belly and arched her brow.

Tristan cried out, "Holy shit you're pregnant. How the fuck did that happen?"

I gave a weak smile. "Oh, you know, birds and the bees and all that."

"Yes," Vincent answered with a curious look. "I'd be interested to know as well. As far as we were aware vampires can't procreate."

I shrugged. "Probably not one of theirs."

"Ah," Tristan bobbed his head with a smirk. "I bet it rubs them raw to find out that their little human servant was the one that knocks you up where they couldn't?"

I scowled at the man. "No, they're fine with it."

Vincent hummed and glanced at his underlings and then back to me. "You know,

I was going to see if you would like to rejoin our little crusade against rogue vampires but it seems as if you will be out of commission for a little while longer. However…”

I didn't like where this was going.

“I would like to propose a different agreement.” Vincent shifted closer to me with a twinkle in his eye. “To ensure the safety of your men and yourself, I would like to have your child as my own.”

I gaped at him. “Uh, what?”

“Yeah, what boss?” Tristan added, his own face aghast at what his president had just suggested.

“Think about it,” Vincent looked to his minions. “We would have a child that comes from two human servants. It would be born with the vampire abilities without the extra negatives that come with it. They would be so much better than just having a single vampire servant. Wouldn't you agree? Then we wouldn't have to worry about those pesky soft feelings towards the vampires that Piper has.”

“You're not getting my baby,” I snapped, moving away from him.

“I don't think you quite understand the position you're in here,” Vincent reminded me, grinning from ear to ear. “You either give me your baby or you give me your life. Either way I'm getting something out of it."

"That wasn't part of the deal," I argued with the urge to wring that man's neck fuck the consequences. "The deal was you get the vampire council and you leave us the fuck alone. You can't back out."

"I can do whatever I want. I'm the president of the hunters guild. They'll do whatever the fuck I tell them to do. If I told them to kill you and take your baby then they will. Right?" he shot back to Mizuki and Tristan.

My eyes moved from Vincent over to the two hunters that I had become sort of friends with over the time of working with them. Would they really do it? Would they really kill me and take my baby just because he said so? I couldn't take the risk.

While Vincent wasn't looking, I raised my stake and prepared to plunge it into his back. Tristan's eyes widened, giving me away. Vincent spun around, his hand catching my wrist. He twisted it until I had to release the stake or break my own wrist.

"I wouldn't do that if I were you," Vincent purred in response with a smug spot expression on his face, knowing that he'd won. "I think I'm going to enjoy having my own child. I've always wanted to be a father.

I've—" his voice cut off a gurgling sound coming out of his throat. A thin red line appeared along his throat. The zinging of Mizuki's blade rang through the air.

Vincent's eyes widened in his hand, let go of mine and reached for his throat. Blood poured out of his neck. The touch was all that his brain needed to realize that he had been hurt and moments away from death his face. Brow scrunched up in a scowl and he fell to his knees and then onto his face his head rolling off to the side next to Caleb's.

I stared at Mizuki. "Why did you do that?"

"I might be a vampire hunter but even we don't hurt kids. I wouldn't wish this life on any of them." She spat on Caleb's and Vincent's body before spinning on her heels and stalking out of the room. She pushed by Antoine and the others on her way out with not so much as a how do you do.

Tristan stared down at Vincent's dead body for a few moments before he too scurried after her.

The guys piled into the room, their eyes searching for me and then finding the dead bodies between us.

"Wow," Drake started with a grin. "Looks like we missed one hell of a party. I knew our girl could take care of herself. He stepped over the dead body of Caleb and wrapped his arms around me, kissing me firmly on the lips. "Did you miss us?"

I chuckled and kissed him back. "You have no idea."

CHAPTER 23

Rayne

I LISTENED INTENTLY TO the minds around us, searching for anyone who had thoughts of coming after us. Most of the hunters were too focused on the vampires they were fighting to even notice that their leader had been killed or that the very person they were coming in here to get was already found.

But there were a few starting to give us an interested look from where I stood in the doorway.

"I don't mean to break up the party but I think we should probably get out of here," I told the others, wanting so much to hold Piper in my arms but knowing that I have to wait until later.

Piper smiled at me and my heart stuttered. "Of course, let's go. Let's get out the hell out of here." She took two steps forward and then grabbed her large stomach groaning out in pain.

"What is it? What's wrong?" Drake, who was closest to her, grabbed one side of her while his brother grabbed the other side of her.

Piper held her stomach and moaned out, "I don't know it just hurts." And then a second later water began pouring out between her legs.

"Uhhh...I'm not an expert," Alister began, pointing out the water puddle on the floor, "but I think she's going into labor. I think her water just broke."

"No shit, Sherlock," Piper shot back at him and then groaned again.

"What should we do? We can't have the baby here," I cried out, shooting my eyes back into the hallway where the vampire hunters were getting a little too close for comfort.

"I had a midwife," Piper began but then her eyes moved over to the other body that was shoved to the side of the doorway. "But I guess she can't help me now."

Antoine took charge. "Let's get out of the building and then we can worry about finding somewhere safe for you to give birth. Do you have any ideas of how to get out of here?"

"We can't just walk out the front door?" Piper asked before leaning against Drake with another groan of pain.

"Because there's a horde of vampire hunters and the vampires they're killing in the way and based on the way they tried to attack us when we were coming in to get you even though they were told not to, I don't trust they are going to leave you alone." If I needed to breathe, I would have been panting after that long winded explanation.

Piper winced and glanced back at the dead body of her midwife. "Well, Agnes said there was an escape route through the basement."

"And where exactly is that located," Antoine asked.

"I have no idea."

"I know," I jumped in before Piper could get upset again. "I've looked at the schematics of the building. Follow me," I told them all before darting into the hallway.

The others followed after me quickly, Drake holding Piper in his arms. We got a few strange looks from the hunters as we passed by but too many of them were focused on their fight to pay attention to us. I darted down to the right, heading back towards the front of the building. There was an entrance to the basement just off of the dining room. Strange that they would set their home up in the same manner that we did.

I quickly found the doorway and ushered us down the stairs, keeping an ear out for any hunters that might decide that it would be a good idea to follow us. I caught sight of Tristan and Mizuki, ushering the others out of the building. With any luck they would be gone before we even got back to the car. I just hoped that Piper would last that long.

"Down here," I instructed them all and they hurried past me, Piper groaning and moaning the entire way. I shut the door behind us, locking it for good measure.

The basement wasn't as well furnished as ours; it was just a big old empty room with a bunch of caskets thrown here and there. The only other object in the room was a large refrigerator lining the wall.

"Where do you think the exit is?" I asked Piper, searching around the room for some kind of hint of a secret passage.

"Why the fuck you asking me? I'm in labor, you idiot."

"Yeah," Drake told me with a snap.

The rest of us quickly went to the walls, pressing here and there searching for an exit to get out of the basement. I could hear the scrimmage upstairs getting worse. It seemed that they couldn't get their hunters to leave. Instead, they were too riled up in their blood lust to listen to their superiors. Especially after they found Vincent's dead body.

"Here it is," Wynn instructed from beside the large refrigerator, pulling it open from one side. "This seems to lead outside."

Without much choice in the matter, we hustled into the doorway. We rushed forward with Piper in between all of us in case we got attacked from either side.

"Do you hear anything else?" Allister asked, coming up behind me.

I listened for voices in my head, for brain patterns that signals someone was around. I shook my head. "No, nothing. Nothing on this side."

"Good," Allister plodded along. "I wonder where this comes out at."

"How about a hospital?" Piper grunt from behind us. "I need a fucking hospital now."

"Piper, try to calm yourself," Antoine assured her. "Stressing yourself out is not going to be good for you or the baby."

"Go stress yourself out you freaking poofy ass motherfucker." Then her whole demeanor changed and she cried out, "Where is Darren?"

"Darren is waiting behind at the house," Antoine answered, not put off by Piper's name calling. "You will see him soon.

"Hey, I think this comes out on the other side of the parking lot," I pointed out as I poked my head out of the door, glancing around the surrounding area. "Look, there's the hunter's car and there's ours. Think we can make it over there?"

"We'll have to," Marcus instructed, taking the lead. "You get Piper to the car and I'll hold them off."

"What?" Piper cried out, grabbing for him. "You can't stay behind, I need you. I need all of you at the hospital with me."

Marcus grasped her hand. "Don't worry. I'll be right behind you."

Before Piper could protest anymore, we rushed towards the car where Marcus headed off anyone who was coming after us. A few vampire servants headed our way with hunters on their tails. I jumped into the driver's seat while the others piled into the back of the car, Allister in the front seat with me.

"Where's the nearest hospital?" I asked anyone in the car.

"Why don't you just GPS it?" Piper commanded from the back seat. "Why do you have to make everything so freaking complicated?"

"Right, exactly," I said, a bit frazzled, grabbing my phone out of my pocket and dropping it on the floor.

"Here, you can just use mine." Alister handed his phone over the nearest hospital already pulled up for me.

"Okay, it's ten minutes away. Can you hold on that long, Piper?" I called to the backseat

Piper screamed out again, "Just fucking drive!"

Putting the car into reverse, I peeled out of the parking lot and zoomed down the road ignoring all traffic laws as I zoomed in-and-out of traffic and towards the hospital. I didn't know if Marcus was going to make it or if he was still back there fighting them off. All I could worry about was getting Piper to the hospital.

"Did you call Darren?" Piper cried out in the back seat. "He needs to know."

"I will message him now," Antoine reassured her, brushing her hair back from her face where she leaned against him.

Those ten minutes were the longest ten minutes of my life.

We pulled into the ER parking and piled out of the car. Drake grabbed hold of Piper under her arms and legs and shouted, "We got a pregnant lady here. Pregnant lady in labor."

"Here's a wheelchair," a nice nurse offered as we rushed into the door.

Drake hissed at her refusing to give over Piper.

"Drake, you must let the lady take care of her. Piper will be fine. The nice doctors will take care of her." Antoine explained to him, placing a hand on his back pushing a bit of his power into his voice so that Drake would listen.

Drake finally lowered Piper into the wheelchair but insisted on being the one to push her. Figuring out that she wasn't going to get anywhere with the man, the nurse led us back to the elevators, which then led to the maternity ward.

"Where's the doctor?" Piper called out, groaning as we helped her on to the bed.

"He'll be a long shortly. We just need to get some information from you. How far along are you?

Piper groaned, her eyes going up to the ceiling. "I don't know seven months, almost eight?" She looked at us as if to get some kind of confirmation.

"Well, when is your due date," the nurse tried again.

Piper shook her head. "I don't know. I don't know. I've been seeing a midwife."

The nurse sighed impatiently. "She should at least given you an approximate due date. Do any of them know what it could be?"

"Unfortunately," Antoine spoke up, "we have not been able to be around during this time. She was being helped by a private company."

The nurse gave us an incredulous look before pulling up a tablet to type something in. "I need one of you to fill out some paperwork. Which one of you can fill out paperwork for her?"

Antoine stepped before her, taking the tablet. "I can handle this. Piper I'll be just outside."

"Yes, okay. Okay. Fine."

"And the rest of them?" the nurse cast a look at the other guys in the room. "Do you want them to wait in the other room as well?"

I stepped up next to Piper's side, grasping her hand in mine. "I'm not going anywhere."

"Well, that's not up to you. That's up to the mother. Who are you comfortable with having in the room?" The nurse asked once more.

Piper groaned and rolled her eyes. "They've all seen me naked. I don't fucking care."

The nurse seemed startled but kept her mouth smartly shut.

A moment later and a short balding older man came in adjusting his glasses on his face. "And what do we have here?"

The nurse brought the doctor up-to-date and he stepped forward to examine Piper. "I'm going to apply a little pressure here. Just want to see how far along you are... oh your cervix is good and softened. I'd say you're about at five so far."

"So, it's time? I can push?" Piper cried out, the hope in her voice making me want to hug her.

The doctor chuckled. "No, not quite yet. You must get to a ten before you can start pushing. And you say her water already broke?"

"Yes," Piper groaned. "It broke everywhere. It was all over the bodies, blood everywhere."

"What?" the doctor asked, concern covering his face. "Blood? There shouldn't be any blood."

"Not my blood," Piper corrected with a sneer.

"Okay," the doctor glanced at us and I shrugged. "Well, I'd say that you're right on time. Your midwife must have been mistaken because I would not say you are in your seventh month." He paused and turned to the nurse. "I'm going to turn things over to the nurse here so she can get you set up with an IV and were you thinking about having an epidural?"

Piper started to answer and I squeezed her hand, leaning down and whispered, "I don't think that's a good idea. It won't work. You heal too fast. It'll push it out before you can even get ready to push."

Piper glared at me and then to the doctor, spitting out, "No. I'm good. I want to do it naturally."

"Are you sure?" The doctor arched a brow at me as if he knew that I was the reason why she had said no and then went back to Piper.

"Yes, I am sure." She forced a smile.

Thankfully, just then Marcus rushed into the room his shirt ripped and blood splattered across his face.

"Oh, thank God," Piper cried out, "you're okay!"

"Excuse me, sir. Are you hurt? Please let one of the nurses check you out," the doctor tried to keep Marcus from coming closer to Piper.

"I'm fine," Marcus pinched out, all his focus on Piper.

"Very well, I'm going to put some of your information in the computer," the doctor sighed and started for the door. "I will be back in a moment." He glanced around the room and I could hear the buzzing of his brain trying to figure out the situation.

"What about Darren?" Piper asked again. "Have we heard from Darren? Is he coming?"

"I'm sure he'll be here and we can ask Antoine when he comes back," Allister reassured her from a distance, he and Drake seemed a little out of their element in the delivery room.

In fact, Drake was looking a bit pale-er.

Piper seemed to notice it too and chuckled before groaning again. "So, bloody guts you can handle but a laboring woman trips you up? Do you want to wait in the waiting room?"

"Please," Drake darted out of the room without another word. His brother followed him shortly after, leaving me with Wynn and Marcus left to be with Piper.

"Anybody else?" Piper asked the room.

Wynn came closer to her and brushed her hair away from her sweaty face, kissing her temple. "I will leave when you wish me to."

"Me too," Marcus announced with the nod of his head, standing next to me.

Antoine walked in once more with the nurse not far behind.

"Everything has been taken care of. Darren is on his way."

"What about Gretchen?" Piper brought up suddenly. "Should we tell Gretchen? Wouldn't she want to be here for this."

Antoine paused and picked up his phone once more. "I'll see what I can do. I can certainly call her."

"Yeah, call Gretchen. I want her here too."

"How much longer do you think she has?" Wynn asked the nurse. She took one look at him and then a second look, her face turning pink at Wynn's attention.

"Any moment now, she's making pretty fast progress now. Faster than any I'd ever witnessed."

"Did you hear that, Piper?" I told her, stroking her brow. "Any time now and we're going to be parents, can you believe it?"

She forced a pained smile at me. "Yup can't believe it. I'd believe it a whole lot more if it wasn't trying to kill me from the inside out."

The nurse chuckled and the rest of us smartly kept our mouths shut. Which was the wise decision when Piper shot an intense glare at the nurse.

"What should we do?" I asked the nurse. "While we wait?"

The nurse shook her head. "There's not much you can do. Keep her company. Help her with breathing. Have any of you had any means of training for delivery? Did you guys go to any kind of Lamaze classes?"

"No, no classes. We were going to do a home birth. You know me, all natural." Piper reinforced that sentiment with a bite of bitterness.

"I have," Marcus spoke up.

We all looked at him in surprise.

"I've helped my sisters deliver their babies."

Piper stared at him. "You have sisters?"

"I did."

"Huh." Just then Piper had another wave of contractions and the conversation was brought to a screeching halt.

"It's okay." The nurse waved to Marcus. "Since you've had experience why don't you stand on the other side of her and help coach her through the breathing. I'm going to get the doctor to come check her out again."

It wasn't more than twenty minutes before Darren appeared in the hospital room doorway.

Piper cried out and reached for him, stopping them mid practice of breathing. "It's Darren! You're here."

"And look who I brought with me," Darren offered her a small smile, gesturing behind him where Gretchen came in followed by the twins and Antoine. It seemed like everyone felt that the time was coming and wanted to be here.

"Oh, my poor baby girl," Gretchen came up to Piper's side, pushing me out of the way to reach her. "What have they gotten you into now?"

Piper grinned up at her through a pained expression. "Oh, you know, just knocked up and everything."

"This is so exciting. I never thought we'd have a baby in the house," Gretchen gleamed overjoyed by the prospect.

"Yup, it's gonna be one full house," Piper retorted, squeezing her hand as another contraction came on.

"Alright, alright. I need a little bit of room in here," the doctor came back into the room with the nurse close next to him. "If you're gonna stay, get out of the way. Who's gonna be with you to help coach you?"

"I will," Marcus nodded his head.

Gretchen glanced at me, shooting a thought my way. I nodded and got out of the way moving to the couch where the others waited.

"I helped my grandbabies be born," she offered Piper in way of an explanation.

"Alright, great, everybody else stay out of the way, so I can check and see if we're ready to go."

Piper seemed to hold her breath while the doctor put his hand underneath her gown once more. A few moments later, he withdrew it and looked up from between her legs. "It looks like it's time. Are you ready to start pushing?"

Piper gasped as a rush of pain took over. "Fuck, yes, get it over with. Get it out of me."

"The things mothers say during labor," the doctor chuckled.

"Oh, this is nothing," Gretchen laughed, "my daughter-in-law had a mouth like a sailor on her when she was giving birth to every single one of her children."

"That's great," Piper grunted out, "but let's focus on me right now."

"Alright, Piper, breathe, one, two, three, push," the doctor instructed while Marcus and Gretchen helped her go through the movements.

Piper's face turned red as she followed the doctor's instructions, veins popping out from under her skin at the strain.

"Alright let's do it again."

"Again? That wasn't it?" Piper blew out with a groan.

"No, not quite. The head's coming but we need to get the rest of them out." The doctor muttered from between her legs.

Piper repeated the procedure with a doctor several more times and then cried out, "Just fucking stake me already. Stake me and get this fucking thing out of me."

I chuckled, coming up next to the doctor. "She's just kidding."

The doctor ignored me and turned back to Piper. "Alright, here we go. One final push and then we're home free."

Piper stared into my eyes while she took a few breaths and then pushed and pushed and then I saw something I never thought I'd see in my lifetime.

It was our baby. It was perfect. It was a girl.

"Would you look at that," Drake glanced over my shoulder at the baby girl the doctor was handing off to the nurse to clean off. "It's a little girl."

"She's beautiful," Allister pointed out, following me and Drake over to where they were cleaning the baby off. Once they were done, they brought the baby over to Piper and offered the baby to her.

Piper, tired and worn out from the experience, took the baby and laid her across her chest and looked down at her. "She's so tiny."

"She looks like you," Drake said with a grin.

"You can't tell that yet," Piper retorted, touching the baby gently as if she would break. "What should we call her?"

The doctor continued to work on Piper quietly, not saying anything while we discussed it amongst ourselves. Of course, no one could agree.

"I don't care. I'm just happy that we have a baby," I told them with a smile on my face. I couldn't stop smiling, it was just so great.

"Whatever you call her, she's gonna have one heck of a time finding anybody to love her more than we do." Allister pointed out, glancing up at the others.

"That is true," Wynn murmured, stepping in next to Marcus, his eyes set on the small child.

Piper hummed and stroked her fingers over the baby as the doctor and the nurses left to give us a moment alone.

"I think I'm too tired to think of a name right now. I just want to sit here and look at her." She peered down at the baby with a soft smile. "Look at all of us. Did you ever imagine that a maid would end up being where I am right now?"

Drake snorted. "I didn't imagine that you'd last the day."

"Oh, come on. She would have lasted longer than that. At least a week," I countered.

"Not with your grumpy ass. You tried everything in your arsenal to get her to leave." Drake pointed with a smirk.

"Come on, let's not fight. This is a happy day," Wynn explained, pushing closer to Piper.

"Yes, it certainly is," Antoine announced, standing near Darren with his arm around his waist. It seemed whatever tension that was between them had been smoothed over by Piper's very presence.

"And you Marcus," Piper asked. "What do you think?"

He stared down at the little girl and said, "I think if she's anything like her mother we'd better hide the vases."

EPILOGUE

Piper

STALKING INTO THE HOUSE, I shouted, "Jack! Your Auntie Mizuki and Uncle Tristan are here!" I glanced over my shoulder at the two hunters and grinned. "Just wait until you see her. She's gotten so big. She'll be so excited to see you two."

I jerked forward, my body propelling toward the ground. I landed on my knees, catching myself on my hands. Stinging pain went through my palms and I growled.

Shifting to the side, I shot a look down at the culprit. Scowling, I grabbed the offending object and pushed to my feet. "Jaqueline Agnes Durand! What did I tell you about leaving your toys in the doorway?"

"Dude, are you okay?" Tristan stopped beside me and stared down at the mess of toys on the floor. "Man, for a maid you don't keep a very clean house."

I glared at him out of the corner of my eye. "Don't even start." A pitter patter of little feet barreled through the house followed by a squeal of delight. I bent down and picked up the array of toys on the floor. "Jaqueline, I mean it. Get over here right now and pick this crap up."

A moment later a raven haired little pixie demon came charging out of the living room. "Uncle Tristan! Aunt Mizuki!" Jack cried out with a beaming smile on her five year old face.

"There's my girl!" Tristan reached down and picked the little hellion up, making her giggle and kick her feet happily.

Mizuki stood by with a small smile on her lips until Jack was done with Tristan and turned to her. Attention span of a gold fish, I swear.

"Auntie Mizuki," she pouted, "Did you not bring me anything?"

The vampire hunter rubbed her chin and hummed. "I don't know. What do you think?" She pulled something from behind her back, holding it out to Jack.

"Is that a...?" I gaped at the woman. "You aren't seriously giving her a stake, are you?"

"Never too early for your first," Mizuki winked at Jack, making her giggle.

Jack turned to me with a quizzical look. "Mommy, what's a stake?"

I flicked a look at Mizuki and mouthed, thanks a lot, before turning back to my daughter. "Why don't you go find Daddy Marcus and ask him?"

Jack pouted for a moment and then perked back up, "Okay!" She charged off once more shouting through the house, "Daddy Marcus! Where are you?"

I sighed and turned back to the two hunters. "I thought when you killed Vincent you wouldn't be making my life any harder?"

Mizuki smirked, flipping her long black hair over her shoulder. "Why would you assume that?"

I locked eyes with her, crossing my arms over my chest and cocking one hip to the side. "We are not playing this game again. I'm done. I have other priorities on my hands now." I uncrossed my arm to show her the toys in my grasp. "Clearly."

"Oh, come on." Tristan pulled one of the toys from my hand, squeezing it so that it made its obnoxious chirping noise. "Don't tell me you don't miss the rush of the fight? The adrenaline rush of slicing the head off a vamp?"

I snatched the toy back from him with a pointed look. "No." Turning away from them, I walked into the living room dropping the toys into the box by the fireplace. "Look, was it fun? Sure. But that was then and don't forget, it wasn't like I wanted to be doing it. Your boss made me, do it."

"Yeah, but now you'd do it 'cause you want to," Mizuki interjected, throwing herself down on the couch, her boots going up on top of the coffee table.

I flicked my eyes down to her feet before shaking my head. "And what would I tell Jack? Hold on while mommy goes and kill people exactly like your daddies?"

"Bad daddies," Tristan pointed a finger at me with a grin.

I wrinkled my nose. "Don't say that."

"So, what are you going to do for the rest of your long, long, long, long, long life?" Tristan went on with a wave of his hand.

"I don't know...be a mom? Be a good girlfriend? Then whatever the hell I want after that. I certainly don't have to spend my nights risking my life and those I love." My body twisted toward the doorway, feeling Antoine before he entered. "Hey, look who decided to visit."

Antoine inclined his head at the two hunters in greeting. He stepped up next to me, placing an arm around my waist and kissing my neck. "Where's Jaqueline?"

I pressed a hand to his chest, playing with the buttons on his shirt. "She's looking for

Marcus. Someone brought her a new toy…” I trailed off, leveling my gaze on Mizuki who simply smirked once more.

“So, Antoine,” Tristan asked, taking a seat across from Mizuki. “Have you heard from the board yet? Did they make a decision?”

Antoine dropped his arm from my waist and stepped forward. “Actually, I just got off the phone with them. It seems that the elections for the new council members will be held in the next week.”

“What?” I gaped at him, my brows shooting up. “You didn’t tell me that.”

“I did not know until just a few moments ago and you were not there for me to tell you,” Antoine explained, arching a brow at me.

“Who’s up for the council?” Mizuki interrupted what was going to be an argument we would deal with later.

Tucking his hands in his pockets, Antoine began describing two vampires I’d never heard of…my brain checked out for that bit only to come rearing back when he said, “And me.”

“Hold up.” I grabbed Antoine by the arm, lowering my voice to a hush whisper. “What do you mean you? Since when are you up for the council position?”

Placing his hands on my arms, he rubbed them up and down in a soothing manner. "I was going to tell you but did not want you to worry until I knew for sure."

"What makes them think you're good enough to be on the council?" Tristan asked without a hint of sarcasm.

Antoine glanced away from me to answer. "It seems that I impressed quite a few people —" I cleared my throat and he added on, "We impressed quite a few people with the dispatching of the previous council, not to mention the incident with Boris. It is quite a feat to take out your own maker and the council in such a short period of time and apparently that means that I am fit for a leadership position."

"Well," Mizuki stood up, stalking over to us. "Let's just hope you can do a better job keeping a tight leash on the vamps around here than the last council did. Because if you don't..." she mimicked staking him in the chest. "Are we clear?"

I pursed my lips and rolled my eyes at her. "Mizuki's kidding. Right?"

She licked her lips and cocked her head to the side. "Am I?"

For a moment, I thought she was serious and then shoved her away with a laugh. "Get out of here. Don't you have a house full of baby hunters who need training?"

Mizuki stretched her arms over her head and cracked her neck. "Yes, it is unfortunate that along with the duties of president I also have to make sure the troops are trained correctly."

"Co-president," Tristan interjected, standing up. "There are five others in charge so we don't get sucked into another crazy tyrant leader again."

"You probably should come up with a different title than co-president," I suggested with a shake of my head. "That's just stupid."

"We're working on it." Tristan placed a hand on Mizuki's arm, earning a scowl from her. "We should get going, can't leave the kiddos alone for too long or they'll burn down the place."

I chuckled. "Don't I know it."

Darren dipped into the room. "Oh, I didn't know we had company."

"Darren, can you show our guests out?" Antoine asked with a meaningful look.

"Of course," Darren bobbed his head and gestured toward the door. "This way please."

Tristan scoffed and shook his head. "Still playing the butler, huh? Doesn't that ever get old?"

Darren's lip tipped up on one side. "There are worse things I could be doing."

"True enough," Tristan nodded and waved to me. "See ya later, Piper. Antoine."

Mizuki left without a word or glance back.

Waiting until the door closed behind them, I turned to Antoine and shoved him on the shoulder. "What the hell? You can't be on the council."

"What is this now?" Darren stepped into the room, his interest peaked. "The council?"

"Antoine is up to be elected to the council," I told Darren with a vigorous wave of my hand. "Tell him he can't."

"Why not?"

I fumbled over my words, stalking toward Darren. "What do you mean, why not? Because it's dangerous, duh. Think about Jack. What if someone decides to get to Antoine through her or one of us? What then?"

"And if he doesn't take the position then we could end up with someone even worse that might decide that we are too much of a threat to let live," Darren explained, placing his hands on either side of my face. "Would you really want to take that chance?"

I placed my hands over his and closed my eyes. So much had happened since I first started this job. I'd lost people and gained people all to get to this point in my life and I was scared. So scared to lose the very people who had made my life worth living and the light of my life. Jack. Oh, little Jack. I would just die if something happened to her.

"No, I can't take that chance." I blew out a breath and Darren kissed me on the forehead.

"That's our girl."

I shifted away from Darren to look at Antoine. "Well, if we're going to do this then let's do this right." I placed my hands on hips and stepped toward Antoine. "Get the guys together, we're going to need a plan. We need Rayne to find out everything he can about the other candidates," I said thinking out loud as I started toward the basement door. "Marcus could do some recon with the twins, make sure that we have the upper hand —"

I paused at the doorway and looked back at the guys with a frown. "Are you coming or what? We've got work to do."

The End

ABOUT THE AUTHOR

Erin Bedford is an otaku, recovering coffee addict, and Legend of Zelda fanatic. Her brain is so full of stories that need to be told that she must get them out or explode into a million screaming chibis. Obsessed with fairy tales and bad boys, she hasn't found a story she can't twist to match her deviant mind full of innuendos, snarky humor, and dream guys.

On the outside, she's a work from home mom and bookbinger. One the inside, she's a thirteen-year-old boy screaming to get out and tell you the pervy joke they found online. As an ex-computer programmer, she dreams of one day combining her love for writing and college credits to make the ultimate video game!

Until then, when she's not writing, Erin is devouring as many books as possible on her quest to have the biggest book gut of all time. She's written over thirty books, ranging from paranormal romance, urban fantasy, and even scifi romance.

www.erinbedford.com